FROM NOW UNTIL FOREVER

LUW ROMANCE CHAPTER

KAYLA HANSEN   STELLA TARYN

DEBRA BIRDWELL WINKLER   JASMINE SIMPSON

JONATHAN REDDOCH   FIO LEFEY   KEYRA K. ALLRED

IRIS MOONFLOWER   SARA FITZGERALD   MAE THORN

MICHAELA RAE   SCARLETT XAVIER

CONTENTS

Get ready to fall in love with the afterlife. *From Now Until Forever* brings together twelve hauntingly romantic stories written by members of the League of Utah Writers' Romance Chapter. This locally crafted paranormal romance anthology is a celebration of passion, loss, magic—and the kind of love that refuses to die.

Triggers: Death/discussions of death, terminal illness (cancer) of a MC, brief depictions of gore.

Celeste

Indigo paint dripped down the canvas where I'd pressed my brush too hard, distracted by the feeling that I wasn't alone in my studio apartment.

"I know you're there."

Everything always felt off after an overnight stay at the hospital, but this was something else.

As soon as I walked through my front door, the already-prepped canvas drew me in. The subject matter of my artwork wasn't markedly different from the images that had dominated my paintings for months since my diagnosis. They'd all been inspired by the things I saw on the streets, which made me question my own sanity.

Though this painting *felt* different... Significant.

My completed projects leaned against the walls around me. They featured a variety of figures from different eras, mismatched with backdrops of modern city streets. Hopefully, my agent would like these better than the last batch, considering I'd left out the gory injuries I usually saw on my chosen subjects.

One canvas showed a woman in a Victorian dress, lace parasol perched over her shoulder. She stood beside a hot dog cart. I'd omitted the bloody handkerchief tucked into her waistcoat.

Another of a boy with a crooked newsie cap plopped on the curb, his cheeks in his hands. Rolled pants revealed worn boots, as he stared at a cracked iPhone in the gutter. Exactly how I'd seen him sitting last week, minus his partially caved in skull.

I'd hoped they all belonged to a horror convention, but I was the only one who saw them. That became apparent when I tried to enlist the aid of a passerby to help the gravely injured little boy, only for the stranger to look at me like I was crazy, ready to call the cops on me, the woman freaking out about a non-existent injured kid.

The more I saw them, the more I realized I was witnessing something I shouldn't be—that something in me had changed. Thanks to the foreign mass consuming the gray matter in my skull, I had begun to see through whatever barrier was supposed to separate the living and the dead.

And the dreams... They'd started the night after I saw the woman in the Victorian dress. Vivid and disquieting—visions of people I'd never met, places and times I'd never experienced, lives I'd never lived. Perhaps I could add hallucinations to my growing list of symptoms, but a little voice insisted this was something else entirely.

I refocused on my newest painting. This ghost wasn't one I'd seen on the streets. Instead, he'd come from my dreams. I'd encountered him several times, speaking a language I didn't know but somehow understood. Behind him always stretched arid seas of sand and a glittering river. He'd guided me onto a small boat nestled amongst dense reeds. I'd trusted him implicitly, and the connection only deepened with each recurrence of the dream.

After looking through my art history books, I realized I dreamed of Egypt.

The backdrop in my painting wasn't pyramids. Instead, it was a splotchy rendition of the corner of my apartment. He looked out of place in front of my dad's old chair, his eyes shining with a gold, different than in my dreams. He seemed to look right through me, tightening a coil in my stomach.

A sharp pang echoed in my brain, a reminder of my tumor's relentless presence. A chilling truth of my inevitable death and there was nothing more to be done. I had opted out of another futile surgery or another round of chemo. Instead, I had come home, arriving with a need to paint the man from my dreams standing in my bedroom.

It was probably a good indicator that I needed to spend more time with real people. My interactions had dwindled to brief nods with my doorman. I'd become adept at pushing everyone else away to shield them from what was coming. Clearly, I was so desperate for connection that I found myself painting an imagined man.

I shook my head, staring at my paint-stained fingers. "Get a grip, Celeste. You're dying, not crazy."

Gideon

My fascination puzzled me. I had a job to do, and yet...

My purpose stood before me, her strawberry-blond hair swept back into a ponytail. Despite lurking in her shadows for days, I'd never revealed myself to her. Regardless, she'd managed an impressive likeness of me in her painting.

She grew more intriguing by the moment.

I'd examined the artwork scattered around her small living space and, unsurprisingly, could tell the veil between life and the beyond was weakening. It often happened to those on the brink of crossing over. Surely, my presence wasn't helping.

Better to finish my task soon.

And yet... I couldn't bring myself to do it. Instead, I nurtured my growing infatuation, a sensation I hadn't felt since I was alive. Watching Celeste kindled a warmth in my eternal body. Her resolve to walk away from the doctors, fully aware of the consequences was breathtaking. The beauty and peace she brought to the Lingerers on my side of the veil through her paintings, stirred something deep within me.

However, none of this changed the strained tether I saw between life and death—the anchor keeping her soul flesh bound. It'd snap soon, and if I didn't fulfill my duty by then, someone else would be sent to claim her.

As long as time flowed, it'd be limited.

She studied her hands, and I wondered what thoughts swirled in her doomed skull.

"Get a grip, Celeste. You're dying, not crazy."

I smiled, yearning to respond. To pierce the unbearable tension that clung to the thin veil separating us. I no longer wished to remain hidden.

"No, not crazy."

Celeste

My heart jolted. As I spun around to confront the voice,

my hip knocked the small table holding my palette, sending it and my brush tumbling.

"Shit!" I reached out, trying to catch them before they splattered everywhere. Suddenly, everything froze.

The table tilted on two legs, my paints half airborne, and the brush dangled impossibly. All sound vanished into eerie silence.

A creak of floorboards broke the stillness, reminding me that I wasn't alone.

I turned slowly, astonished to see what I'd already painted.

He stood there—the man I'd dreamed about and captured on canvas. His attire didn't match the old linen tunic from Egypt but mirrored my painting, clad in black that melded with the shadows at his feet.

His confident smile complemented his defined features. A curl of onyx hair draped across his brow, his olive skin glowing in the sunset-orange light streaming through my sliding glass door. Shadows danced along the floor between us, as if night seeped through the crystalline wind chime on my porch rather than sunlight.

"You're not afraid." Not a question. He already knew.

I huffed, struggling with my own lack of reaction. Seeing him evoked comfort and a strange excitement. "I guess not."

I felt I already knew him, though admitting it seemed ridiculous. He watched me, as if aware of my thoughts and waiting for me to voice them.

Nothing to lose, I guess.

"I've seen you in my dreams. I didn't think you were the one watching me."

"And whom were you expecting?" He stood like a statue.

I'd hoped he'd focus on the dream comment. "I don't

know. The Grim Reaper?" I eyed his hands clasped behind his back. "Hiding a scythe?"

He smirked and withdrew his hands, revealing his empty palms. "Part of the branding, but not necessarily a required tool."

My gut clenched. "So, you *are* the Grim Reaper?"

"Not '*the*.' I'm one of many. Just '*a*' reaper. Gideon."

"So I've been dreaming about a reaper? Named Gideon?"

He hesitated before moving, his steps graceful as he approached the canvases leaned against the wall. "What do you see in your dreams?"

He examined my paintings with care, and I wondered if maybe this was a hallucination. An arrogant one, if a reaper could truly be interested in my art.

But God help me, I told him about my dreams.

Gideon

She was more extraordinary than I imagined.

I'd heard stories about those close to the veil catching glimpses of past lives, drawn by the ever-whirling energies rippling within the invisible curtain.

In my monitoring, I must have gotten too close, allowing her to make a connection and granting her a glimpse into my past instead of just her own.

Drawn to her paintings of the Lingerers, I'd developed a strange sense of gratitude for her being able to take away their suffering in her depictions. I had been present for many of their deaths, and she made them appear more at rest than they ever seemed to me.

My hands paused half way through a stack of canvases. Examining a landscape, I was struck with nostalgia. Carefully, I freed the art piece from the pile, taking it reverently in both my hands.

A tree dangerously close to the edge of a fjord cliff. The waters below glistened, a ghostly glacier carving through the distant mountains. She'd added two small figures beside the tree, their backs turned, as if taking in the breathtaking scenery. Hands clasped between them.

And I knew the glacier.

Being a reaper, I had certain privileges, including knowledge that Celeste seemed to be breaking through to on her own—who she might have been before. But I needed to know for certain.

"Tell me about this one."

Celeste's brow furrowed, a charming expression of confusion and curiosity. She shrugged as she took a step toward me. An unexpected move. Most would have been terrified of a stranger appearing in their locked apartment.

"Another dream. I'd been watching Vikings that night, so there might've been some inspiration there."

"You dreamed you were a viking?"

A rosy blush surfaced. "Doesn't everyone dream about being a powerful warrior, sometimes?"

After carefully returning the painting to the pile, I turned to her. "Not everyone, Celeste. Nor are they dreaming the way you are."

"How am I dreaming?" She didn't recoil, and I heard her gentle inhale as I stepped closer. She was just as curious about me as I felt about her. And knowing she could see me— allow me to be near— sent electricity through me. As if my body, even as it was, sensed something my mind didn't understand yet.

"You're seeing the past. Memories of lives lived."

"They're memories? Whose?"

Egypt. The fjord. Both memories of my own. However, I shared those moments with another.

"It's possible you're picking up on the lives of the Lingerers you've witnessed. Or myself. Or..." The more I thought about it, the more hopeful I became.

"Or, what?"

"They could be your own. Lives experienced before this one." The yearning for it to be true made my heart thrum. "I can help you remember more clearly if you'd like."

She gave me a quizzical look. "You would do that? I'd think there were rules against that or something."

Or something. But I needed to know.

I stepped into her, expecting her to back away, but she stood strong as I moved close enough to feel her breath tickle my collar. Lifting my hand to her cheek, I felt her warmth radiate through me. Instead of flinching away, Celeste's eyes closed briefly, lips parting to take a steadying breath. She felt whatever magnetism I sensed as well.

"Are you ready? It will be a lot to take in."

She pursed her lips and nodded against my palm.

Celeste

Images suddenly flooded my mind, making my soul tingle. But they weren't flat memories. Instead, joy and sorrow from every experience flooded into me like a great tidal wave. Sucking in a sharp breath, my cheeks heated as warm tears began to stream down them. But I couldn't recall exactly why I was crying. So many different life experiences felt impossible to comprehend and shock rattled through my bones, punctuated by each ending of each life I now remembered.

My knees buckled, but strong arms tightened, holding me

up. Gideon pulled me against his chest, and I buried my face against him. Hot tears soaked into his black shirt before I could question why I welcomed his comfort.

Gideon's face was a common occurrence in my memories. I remembered every time I had tried to brush that stubborn curl from his forehead, only for it to fall perfectly back into place.

I had so many questions. But pressed against him, I felt the first real peace I had in a long time. I knew the depth of the man he was without truly understanding how. Squeezing my arms around him, I fought to control the confused sobs rushing through me. His embrace only grew firmer.

"What do you remember?"

"So much." I choked, trying to find the words. "I knew you—*know* you." I marveled at the serendipity of it. In every memory, in every lifetime, we had always found each other. Or at least we had until...

"Virginia." The memory of the old farmstead and distant cannon fire felt like only yesterday. I'd kissed Gideon hard, tugging on the collar of his dirty blue uniform, the brim of his kepi digging into my forehead. I'd begged him to come home safely. But after the gray clad Confederates had retreated through our cornfields, he hadn't come back to our doorstep. "You died on that battlefield."

Gideon pulled back, gently catching my chin and guiding my eyes up to his. They spoke of apologies he'd never been able to say before. "I wanted to return to you. But that death changed everything and I was offered an opportunity to become what I am."

A surge of anger boiled in my chest. "Why would you accept it? We might have found each other again." Instead, I recalled being alone in every subsequent life. Even this one had proven lonely despite a few half-hearted relationships.

The tumor only exacerbated the problem. However, at the look of regret and sadness in Gideon's golden eyes, my anger quickly subsided.

"Without the knowledge of our shared memories, I couldn't have known. The reaper who greeted me in death told me the offer was an honor—a gift in exchange for my valor on the battlefield. Eternity and an end to suffering. I only wish we had more time together now."

I looked around at my unmoving surroundings. "You've frozen time, though."

"Not for much longer. I'm afraid of another coming for you."

It made sense in the grand scheme. Death couldn't be avoided or there'd be cosmic consequences, if every story ever told were to be believed. If he didn't finish the job, someone else would.

I squeezed his arms, looking up at him. "Find me in the next life, then. There will be another, right? Just don't wait until I'm dying and help me remember."

"Celeste." Although my name sounded sweet coming from his lips, his tone sank. He wouldn't be able to. Some reaper rule, I was sure. The idea of another life without him left a hollow ache in my gut. For the first time in months, I felt fear for what came next.

His fingertips brushed featherlight along my jaw. "Believe me, knowing what I do now, I would never have taken the offer."

I looked up at him. "Can you give it up?" Guilt roiled in my stomach, but need fueled my tongue. "Maybe it can be like it used to be, and we can find each other in the next life?"

Gideon tensed, his eyes growing distant for a moment. "I never..." He hesitated. "This was a gift for my sacrifice. But perhaps—"

In a blink, he vanished, leaving his sentence unfinished.

The palette clattered to the floor, the small table landing with a thud mimicking my heart.

I couldn't be sure if his sudden departure was of his choosing or not. Perhaps a new reaper would appear in my apartment any moment.

I eyed the mess, then let my gaze rise to the painting of Gideon. Still perfectly mysterious, my longing having grown exponentially. But he was gone as suddenly as he'd appeared, and the void within me began to open like a maw.

Had I really expected something different? Though I could recall every moment of the lives he'd revealed to me, could it all have been a giant hallucination? Nevertheless, my thoughts drifted back to that final moment on the porch of the farmstead, my lips against his.

I sucked in a breath. I didn't want to cry anymore.

A sudden pressure on my hips made me yelp. The familiar touch eased the surprise, and I turned to see Gideon before me again. He looked different, his eyes gleaming with certainty. He chuckled as he pulled me close. "Sorry. I didn't mean..."

I smacked him in the chest but gratefully relented to his embrace. I could hear the chirps of the birds outside and the low hum of my AC unit. Time still moved on, and I didn't know what that meant yet.

"Where did you go?"

"It doesn't matter. But my sacrifice on that battlefield does." He brushed his fingers down my arm. "I've missed you. I'd like more time. Now."

I leaned into his touch. "You said that wasn't possible? That someone else would come."

"I've changed all that." He pulled me close, his hips tight against mine.

I hesitated, trying to understand what he was saying. "How?"

He touched my jaw. "Kiss me, first."

My mind went back to Virginia. But he wouldn't be leaving and dying after a kiss this time. I would.

Gideon must have sensed my thoughts because he shook his head and smiled warmly. "Trust me."

And I did, with every fiber of my being. Our lips met and fire rushed through me as his mouth moved against mine. The familiarity of him allowed us to find the rhythm we both knew and craved. His tongue brushed my lip and I wanted more, hungrily taking everything he was willing to give.

The room around me blurred, and time seemed to cease again. The sharp pinprick in my skull brought me back, a ringing in my ears forcing me to pull away. I winced, and waited for the world to turn black.

But Gideon held me. His lips formed a firm kiss against my forehead, and the ringing ceased. My head felt oddly numb for a moment, but then it passed.

"What was that?"

Gideon smiled and it made my head feel light. The gold rims of his irises began to fade, his eyes returning to the familiar, more human, brown I remembered from every life before.

"It's over now. We will have *this* lifetime and the next. I gave it all, for you."

His mouth claimed hers, warm hands tangling up into her hair.

She hummed against his lips, daring now to dream of tomorrow.

YOU TURN ME UP
STELLA TARYN

"Oh, Benjamin. Not again."

I sigh the heaviest of ethereal sighs as I watch my charge gently pry... Randy's?... Rowdy's?... Rudy's?... arm from his naked torso and slip from the bed. Ben snatches his boxers off the floor and briefly looks for the rest of his clothes before remembering they came off in the living room. And the hallway. And the foyer. He tiptoes into the hall, barely breathing in his effort to escape the room undetected. He gathers his clothes as he makes his way to the front door and slips out into the night. Poor Rory(?) doesn't even stir.

"I was hopeful about this one," Ari says.

"Me too," I sigh again. "He was so... happy."

"And present," Nori adds.

"And..." I search for the word.

"Free," Ari says solemnly. "He was free."

Yes. He was *free*. Cue all the sighs in the universe.

I try to remember whose house we're fleeing as Ben wrestles his clothes back on in the cab of his truck and begins the long drive to Cedar City from... Ricky's?... house in St. George.

You'd think I'd remember this guy's name. I am a spirit

guide, after all. It seems like I should know it, being unbound from the limitations of an Earthly existence and all. But I'm what you'd call a... medium-vibration entity. Or, like medium-low? Definitely not *low*-low. Medium-low. Absolutely.

Anyway, the lower a spirit guide's vibration (and to be clear, I still vibrate at a way higher frequency than your average human... okay, maybe not *way* higher, but like, noticeably higher), the more tethered they remain to human-made constructs like time. So even though Ari would say this moment contains all the moments and there's no such thing as remembering or not remembering... or something?... right now, I cannot, for the eternal, unbound-by-Earth life of me, remember this dude's freaking name. I'm certain I knew it when our Benny boy got into the man's bed. But I can't remember it now and that means one thing: Ben's shame is dripping all over me.

Ari, who reminds me often that they are a *high-vibe* spirit guide, doesn't get bogged down in shame. They vibrate high above it, I guess.

"Ari," I finally groan. "I can't remember his name."

"The shame again?" they say knowingly, but not unkindly. "It's Richard."

"Ricky! I knew it!" I'd high-five myself if I still had arms.

My celebration is short-lived as Benjamin miserably winds his way along the highway, taking him further from Richard and closer to the life that told him Richard is the wrong kind of person to love. His shame is nearly drowning me. Ari says this is my most important lesson in spiritual guidance: to learn to out-vibrate my human's shame. (They say I'm still too close to my own human experience, but I can learn. *Ugh.* I'm trying.)

Benjamin tries, too. Sometimes he attempts to move

faster than the shame. Tearing off clothes, licking and sucking and pulling fast and hard, hoping the frantic panting will drown out the words that plague him: *You're disgusting. You're unnatural. You don't belong here.* It doesn't work. They never go away.

Sometimes, he moves slow. Hoping that if he focuses on the pleasure, on taking care of his partner, it will feel different. He'll be connected. He'll feel something closer to the love he craves, the love he can never find with the girls he's tried to date. He only feels lonelier and more broken, even before it's over.

But, oh, last night. When Benjamin sidled up to the bar and met Richard's eyes, he felt something loosen in his chest, even as something else sparked bright and hot. He forgot to be ashamed, or lonely, or desperate for relief. He let himself get lost in Richard's kind eyes and gentle touches as they talked and laughed, glimpsing what love could feel like if only he were free.

He went home with Richard, surrendering to every want, every need he'd ever buried deep. He let Richard love him, just as he was, for a few hours. Then he awoke in the dark with Richard's arms around him and remembered to hate himself again.

Nori is determined to cheer him as he races up I-15, further and further from Richard's bed. Nori was Benjamin's dog until he was six years old, but even when she died she couldn't leave him. She floats around him while he grips the steering wheel, vibrating her doggy spirit goodness all over him. By the time he gets to Cedar, there's a tiny sliver of hope peeking out from beneath the shame. Nori ruffles his hair—which she does all the time, though he rarely feels it—just as he's driving past the coffee shop on Main. She doesn't say anything to Ari or me, but I feel a strange tug at that moment, too. A tug toward something true and beautiful inside that shop.

The woman behind the counter startles when Ben walks in. She's wearing faded jeans and a knit tank top. Her hair is long and blond, half pulled into a knot at the back of her head.

"Whoa. Okay. Rough morning?" Her voice is teasing. She cocks an eyebrow and watches Benjamin with sparkling eyes.

"What?" He glances down to discover his fly is down, his t-shirt is inside out, and his navy plaid button-down is, well, buttoned down all wrong. If there were a mirror nearby, he'd see that his hair is fucking *wild* right now. He looks back at the barista with panicked, bloodshot eyes.

Her face softens into a tender smile. "Do you know what you want, or should I just make you something with all the caffeine in Iron County?"

One corner of Benjamin's mouth tips up. "All the caffeine, please. Thank you."

"Any flavor requests? Hazelnut? Salted caramel? Hope for a better tomorrow?"

The other corner ticks up. "Surprise me."

She beams at him. "That's my specialty."

"I think it might be," Benjamin mumbles, pulling out his wallet.

That's when I notice how close I am to the counter.

Normally, Ari and I keep to the edges of a space like this. Ari is teaching me to keep my metaphorical eyes on the whole of Benjamin's experience, especially in public spaces. We hover by doors and windows so we can run interference with any entities mucking about that won't serve Benjamin's highest good and coordinate with other spirit guides to keep our charges protected. Nori stays close to Benjamin's side—

even in spirit form, a golden retriever does what a golden retriever does—but Ari is showing me how to focus on the macro, not the micro.

So why am I here—like, *right here*—while Benjamin orders his coffee? As soon as I ask the question, I feel her. She's hovering just to the right of the barista.

"Hi," I say, and if I had lungs, I'd be breathless.

"Hi. Is he yours?"

"Yes. That's Benjamin. I'm Quinn."

"Quinn."

I feel my vibration elevate at least ten percent when she says my name.

"Is she yours?" I ask, referring to the barista.

"Yes," she beams and her warmth is like the sun. "That's Skye."

"And you? What are you called?"

"Hope."

"Hope and Skye." My whole being smiles. "Beautiful," I murmur, soaking in the brilliance of Hope's presence. I'm weak in the metaphorical knees.

"One extra large hazelnut latte with a bonus espresso shot reporting for duty." Skye slides the cup across the counter to Benjamin alongside a white paper bag.

"Oh. I didn't order any food." Ben tries to slide the bag back toward Skye.

She laughs. "It's a breakfast sandwich. No offense, but I think you need some protein. It's on the house."

"Thanks," Ben mumbles and trudges to his truck. I reluctantly follow, leaving Hope behind.

It's easy to get Benjamin back there the next day. A few whispers in his ear just before he wakes, and thirty minutes later, I'm with Hope again, watching Skye slowly crack away at Benji's sadness. Her gentle teasing—"so that's what you look like when you've showered"—has him smiling in spite of himself, and this time he stays to drink his latte.

Hope is even more radiant now. She stays close to Skye, enveloping her in love and warmth, and I swear I see it beam right out of Skye and straight into Benjamin. It's like Hope is guiding both of them, and it's so, so beautiful. She shows me how she does it, and I spend the rest of Benjamin's visit practicing. I have to raise my vibration again and again to keep Benjamin surrounded. By the time we leave, I'm exhausted... and sated.

The next day, Hope hovers on the periphery with Ari and me, pointing out the entities who frequent the cafe and introducing the spirit guides of Skye's regulars. We join forces to surround the entire space with love, joy, and gratitude. I feel connected and powerful. It's intoxicating. I never want to leave Hope's side.

Now I have to make sure Benjamin never wants to leave Skye's.

Is that wrong? How could it be? Benjamin is *happy*. Well, except when he's sad... which is every time he thinks of Richard, and what they might have had if he were brave enough to unleash the truth buried inside him.

"Would you have dinner with me tonight?" Skye asks Benjamin one morning.

Ben squirms and clutches his cup tighter. "Like, um, like a date?"

Skye rolls her eyes, smiling fondly. "Yes, Ben, like a date. I'd like to go on a date with you."

Benjamin's eyes widen, and he swallows hard. "I, uh..." he starts, and I have no choice but to intervene. I'm doing this for him. I'm encouraging him to connect with another human being, to accept affection and tenderness. I swirl around him, holding him tight, willing him to feel me, to hear me.

"Yes," I whisper in his ear. "Say yes to Skye."

He blinks twice and listens to his spirit guide. "Yes. Let's have dinner."

I feel Ari watching me the rest of the day, but Ben and Skye are halfway through their date before Ari finally speaks.

"Quinn."

I prickle with defensiveness. "Why are you saying my name like that? All disapproving? Isn't disapproval super low frequency?"

When they don't answer, I continue, "You know what's super high frequency? *Gratitude.* You should be grateful our boy is on a date with someone who's kind to him, who's good for him."

Ari is unmoved. "He's gay."

"Maybe he's bisexual. Or pansexual. Maybe he mostly likes men, but could be just as happy with the right woman... like Skye."

Ari studies me. "He is absolutely gay, Quinn. We must help him love beyond what he's been taught, to find freedom in who he is and who he wants to be with. You know this, and you pushed him toward Skye. Tell me why."

"You know why."

"I want to hear you say it."

If I had a body, I'd be squirming. "He seems happier around Skye. I want him to be happy." If I had eyes, I'd refuse to look Ari in theirs.

"And?"

"Don't make me say it," I whisper.

"Quinn."

"I want Hope," I admit. "I want her forever."

I brace myself for Ari's disappointment, for heavy sighs and high-vibe admonishments for putting my needs above my charge's. I expect an immediate whooshing back to Earth to learn more lessons before I can give this spirit guide thing another try.

I sense Ari move closer. And closer. And closer. Until Ari is... all around me, above me and below me, in front of and behind me, on me and inside me. Their voice is everywhere and nowhere when they say, "Watch how it all turns out."

For the first time, I vibrate beyond time.

———

For Benjamin, who remains very much connected to time, it takes ten days and three dates to muster the courage to kiss Skye, another week to decide he doesn't mind it, two months and a handful of mental pep talks to invite her to his bed (that's a story for another day), and nearly three months to convince himself that this will be enough for him. A few days after that, it all falls apart.

But I knew this moment was coming.

"What is the matter with you?" Hope asks as we watch Ben and Skye wait outside the restaurant where they're meeting her brother.

If I had a stomach, it would be in knots. If I had arms, they'd be holding a bucket and I'd be heaving the contents of said stomach into it. How can a non-corporeal spirit be nauseous? I don't know, but I am. Knowing how the movie ends does *not* make the middle any easier to watch (follow me for more spiritual truths).

"I... uh... wait. Do you not know what's about to happen?" Hope for sure vibrates higher than me. I assumed she'd seen this movie already, just like Ari.

"I know it all turns out."

"Right, but *this* moment is about to be terrible."

Hope laughs. "I know she'll be okay. I don't worry about

the specific moments along the way. Whatever happens, I'll love her through it."

Damn, this girl. Or this feminine-energy spirit. Whatever. She rocks my world. I'll never get enough.

"Here he is!" Skye beams as she pulls her brother into a tight hug. "Ricky, this is my boyfriend, Ben."

Benjamin's breath catches, his eyes widening in shock. "Richard?" he murmurs.

Richard has turned to stone. My spirit dry heaves.

"You know each other?" Skye asks.

Benjamin's shame rises hard and fast, swamping me, trying to swallow me whole. I'm suddenly heavy, fuzzy, weak.

"I've got you." Hope is beside me. "Stay focused. Stay with Benjamin. Vibrate higher. That's it. You can do this. Love him beyond this, Quinn. Help him see."

I focus on Hope's voice as I raise, raise, raise my vibration. My frequency goes higher than it's ever gone before, anchored and buoyed all at once by Hope's presence.

"Yes, yes, yes," she chants around me. Ari adds their voice to the chorus of encouragement. I feel Nori, too, all warmth and playful energy, raising me up, up, up.

We're all there—Ari and Nori and Hope and another beautiful presence I assume is one of Richard's guides but I'll introduce myself later—vibrating higher and louder and truer than the shame. We drown it out, push it out and away from Benjamin and Richard and sweet, sweet Skye who already knows her heart's about to be broken.

Benjamin turns to Skye with watery eyes. "I'm sorry. I'm so sorry." He grasps her hands. "I... we..."

"We went out a few months ago," Richard fills in, looking between his sister and her boyfriend with anguished eyes.

Skye gapes at Ben. "You're bi? Or... gay?"

Ben flinches at the word, but there's no malice in it. Only curiosity and hurt.

He's never said it out loud. Not once. He swallows around the thickness in his throat. He squeezes her hands tighter.

"I..." A sob breaks loose, swallowing his voice.

We hold our vibration high, singing louder than his shame. *You are loved, Benjamin. You are whole. You are free.*

Tears spill down Ben's cheeks. "Yes," he finally chokes out. "I'm gay. I'm gay. I'm gay." He says it three times, like he's clicking his heels, willing himself home. He falls into Skye's arms, clutching her tight while he sobs. Richard watches with trembling lips and streaming eyes.

"I knew she'd be kind," I say to Hope. "Even if Ari hadn't shown me what would happen, I sensed she would never hurt him. And I'm so happy he'll be with Richard now."

"Hmm," Hope hums. "He might be."

"But I already know he will. Ari showed me."

"Ari showed you how it *might* turn out. How it could turn out. It is one of many possible futures."

Record scratch. "Wait. *What?*"

"Ari showed you it was okay that you pushed Ben into dating Skye. That it could still lead to Benjamin's highest good."

"But... but Ari showed me that Skye would lead Benjamin back to Richard—albeit in the most unbelievably awkward way—and you could switch siblings and we would still be together. Hope, please. Please tell me that's what happens. Tell me we'll get to be together."

"We are together."

"But I mean always. Like forever-together. Even when Skye and Ben break up."

"Right now is forever, Quinn."

"OMG is this puzzle night at the Spirit Guide Disco? I don't understand!"

I feel Hope draw nearer, and it's just like when Ari took me beyond time. She's around me and in me... and suddenly she *is* me.

"This moment lives inside you." Her voice is everywhere. "You and I, we live forever. Our love, it's here. Right Now. Always."

I feel it. I feel her. I see it all, every timeline Benjamin could have chosen, and every one he could yet still choose. Every future that leads him back to Richard's door. There are so, so many of those. There are futures that lead to someone else's door, where Benjamin's choices find him a different man to love. There are futures where Benjamin never chooses a man at all, where he lets the shame back in and never breaks free. There are fewer of those, and they grow fuzzier as I watch, less likely, while the futures with a free and joyful Benjamin—a loved and loving Benjamin—pull more sharply into focus.

In every possible future, I feel Hope inside me, loving me. She's in every moment because this moment contains all the moments that ever were, ever will be, and ever could be. She's mine, right now and forever.

Together, we vibrate beyond time.

AFTERWARDS
DEBRA BIRDWELL WINKLER

"It was a dark and stormy night..."

"Not that overused phrase, sister," said Aunt Betsy, her fingers poised above the typewriter keys. "We're not writing a scary story."

Aunt Beth Anne retorted, "Well, why not use it? It's an excellent opening line. Several authors have thought the same."

"It's a contentious phrase," Aunt Betsy claimed, dropping her hands to her lap. "Lord Lytton used it in his novel, *Paul Clifford*. Edgar Allan Poe took it from Lytton and Madeleine L'Engle began her book, *A Wrinkle in Time*, with the same phrase. Even Ray Bradbury used it."

"This isn't your English classroom and I'm not one of your students."

Aunt Betsy stood. "If you were..."

"Sisters, please. That's enough!" Aunt Bertie snapped. She stood patiently waiting by the open French doors. "It's time. Look, she's here!"

Aunt Betsy and Aunt Beth Anne immediately joined Aunt Bertie at the doors. Together, they rushed forward to greet a young woman who was shielding her eyes with her hand.

"Welcome!" the sisters chorused.

Aunt Bertie called, "Hello sweet Sonya."

Aunt Betsy smiled. "We've been waiting for you."

Aunt Beth Anne added, "You're right on time."

Sonya glanced around and asked, "Where am I? It's bright here with no clouds in the sky above."

"Are you okay, dear?" Aunt Betsy asked with concern.

"I was just on my way to work and..." Sonya stared at the three women. Then, she relaxed. "Wait, I know you."

"Of course, you know us, dear." Aunt Bertie smiled.

"You're my three great-aunts!" Sonya confirmed.

"We've been waiting right here to greet you," Aunt Betsy said.

"Come, Sonya. We'll show you around." Aunt Bertie hooked her elbow into Sonya's.

Aunt Betsy pointed to buildings on the left. "That's the gym and the theatre."

Aunt Beth Anne pointed to the right. "There's the library and next to it is the community center where we play Bingo."

Sonya laughed. "I remember our playing Bingo together when I was just a kid!"

The three sisters grinned.

"Good," Aunt Bertie said. "I'd love for you to join us for Bingo after you get used to the place."

Aunt Beth Anne pursed her lips. "In the meantime, maybe you can help us with a story we're writing. 'It was a dark and stormy night,' is the first line."

Aunt Betsy chimed in, "I explained the line's been used too many times.

Sonya giggled. "I agree, the line is overused."

"I don't want another opening line," Aunt Beth Anne fumed. "And, now, I'm not sure how to write this story."

Sonya was intrigued. "I didn't know you were writers."

Aunt Bertie smiled. "Of course we are. We entertained your mother with our stories when she was a little girl."

"I loved hearing your stories when I was little. I didn't know you wrote them."

"Of course we wrote them," Aunt Bertie confirmed.

Aunt Beth Anne crossed her arms over her chest. "And with our new story, I am sure that English Lord Whatever-His-Name-Was won't be offended if we use his phrase."

"Aunt Beth Anne, Lord Edward Bulwer-Lytton was a poet, historian, novelist, playwright, and member of Parliament. I based my teaching master's thesis on him," Sonya commented.

"Sounds like a pompous bastard, if you ask me," Aunt Bertie claimed. "Never trust a Brit."

"But my father was from London," Sonya said, surprised. "You liked him."

"She's got you there, Bertie," Aunt Beth Anne replied.

Aunt Betsy cleared her throat. "You don't like Brits because of Neville."

"Who's Neville?" asked Sonya, inquisitively. "An old boyfriend?"

"Not a boyfriend," Aunt Beth Anne whispered behind her hand. "Fiancé. His plane was shot down during the war."

Aunt Bertie stamped her foot. "Enough! I'm not the one being discussed!"

Aunt Betsy and Aunt Beth Anne froze next to their niece.

Finally, Sonya broke the silence. "So, will someone tell me why I'm here with you three?"

Aunt Bertie put her hands on her hips and gave Sonya a long stare. "It's our job to help you with your future, dear."

"My future?" Sonya stymied her aunts. "Why is my future your business?"

Aunt Betsy smiled. "Sonya, you know we love you and we want your future to be happy."

"Why meddle in my life?" Sonya eyed each of her three aunts. "I earned my degrees, have a marvelous job, and bought a great condo overlooking the city's flower garden and arboretum. What more could I want?"

"What happened to that nice attorney?" Aunt Beth Anne asked sweetly.

Sonya sighed, "Aunt Beth Anne that was three years ago, and he decided to marry someone else."

"How rude," Aunt Betsy jeered.

"I couldn't agree more," Sonya answered sadly.

"Who were you just dating?" Aunt Betsy inquired.

Sonya gave a weak smile. "A few months ago, I broke up with a cute pilot. I thought we were right for each other, but I found out he was married."

"That's so sad," remarked Aunt Beth Anne.

Sonya faced her aunts and informed them with clarity. "I'm twenty-nine, and after dating various professional and non-professional guys, I've decided I am quite enough for me and am really happy right now."

"Sonya, we only want what's best for you," Aunt Bertie said.

"You are beautiful and alone you should not be," confirmed Aunt Betsy.

"I absolutely agree," echoed Aunt Beth Anne.

Sonya questioned, "Are you saying I can't take care of myself?"

"Never said that," Aunt Beth Anne whispered.

"You're saying I need a man to be complete?"

Aunt Bertie wrapped an arm around Sonya and said, "I know what will cheer you up! Let's go for a walk in the park. There's the most beautiful garden you've ever seen on the other side."

They walked in the park without a word.

Aunt Bertie sat on a wooden bench and patted the seat next to her. "Sit here, dear."

Sonya reluctantly obeyed Aunt Bertie, while the other aunts sat on either side.

"Now, then," Aunt Bertie said, taking Sonya's hand in hers. "We want you to meet this nice guy..."

"No, no, no," Sonya said, jerking her hand from Aunt Bertie's grasp and shaking her head. "And, again, I say NO!"

Aunt Bertie said, "We're here to help you, Sonya. So, just listen. This nice young man..."

Sonya looked for support from Aunt Betsy and Aunt Beth Anne, but both shot her looks which reminded her of when she was in trouble as a child.

"... who is a year older than you and arrived this morning"

"He's the grandson of our friend, Sheila," Aunt Betsy said. "We all play Bingo together."

"She's a very nice lady and we have known her for... well, since we... ah... first met her." Aunt Beth Anne struggled with the right words.

"He's an architect named Boone and Sheila says he's a really nice young man."

"Really, Aunt Bertie? A nice young man named Boone?" Sonya scrunched up her face. "What kind of name is Boone?"

"He was named for his grandfather, Sheila's husband," Aunt Bertie let Sonya know. "You have similar interests, and an architect and a teacher make a good match."

Sonya declared, "I don't need a matchmaker."

"Please just meet him, Sonya," Aunt Betsy pleaded.

"Humor us and meet Boone, please." Aunt Beth Anne added.

"If he doesn't work out," said Aunt Betsy, "there are several young men at Bingo."

"The three of you never married, so why should I?" Sonya protested.

The aunts looked at each other. Then, Aunt Betsy spoke, "The pickings were pretty slim when we were of marriageable age, Sonya."

Aunt Beth Anne added, "The war took a lot of the boys from our town, you know. Didn't leave enough options to go around."

Aunt Bertie sternly looked at her niece. "Sonya, that was then, and this is now."

The four women sat without speaking as if time had stopped.

Ultimately, Sonya took a deep breath. "Fine. Will you leave me alone if I agree to meet this Boone character?"

"We promise," Aunt Betsy and Aunt Beth Anne said in stereo.

"And he's not a Brit." Aunt Bertie was rather proud of that fact.

Sonya snickered. "Well, I now know why you approve of him, Aunt Bertie."

Her aunts led Sonya towards an elegant garden of roses, azaleas, and camellias of white, pink, red, and yellow. There were irises and daisies along the walkway into the garden and beyond, orange, lemon, and Japanese cherry trees. A dark and tall handsome man stood nearby the entrance arbor decorated with climbing pink, red, and yellow roses. He had dark hair with bits of gray at his temples and his delightful smile charmed Sonya, immediately.

She blushed as she faced her aunts. "Is this Boone? He looks rather nice, has a friendly smile, and dresses well."

"He does, doesn't he?" Aunt Bertie whispered. "Why don't you two take a stroll in the Garden of Eden, Sonya."

"Garden of Eden?" Sonya questioned.

The aunts nodded.

"Any snakes?"

"Of course not," Aunt Beth Anne said.

Aunt Betsy chuckled, "The exterminator was here last week."

"Go now, Sonya," Aunt Bertie encouraged. "We'll catch up to you later."

Sonya smiled as she walked towards the handsome man. "Hello, you're Boone, right?"

"Yes, and you must be Sonya," he replied in a deep baritone.

"My aunts told me you're an architect," Sonya said.

"Yes, I am," Boone assured her.

"And single?"

Boone nodded his head. "My gran told me you're single as well."

"Yes," Sonya murmured.

"I must say," Boone began, "my gran told me you were pretty, but you are beautiful."

"Thank you, Boone," Sonya said. "My aunts said you were handsome, and I must agree."

The two smiled.

"I understand my gran plays Bingo with your aunts."

"That's what they tell me."

"Do you like Bingo?" Boone inquired.

"When I was a youngster, my aunts took me to our local

community center on Sunday afternoons." Sonya blushed. "I haven't played in years."

"So, you like the game?"

"Yes," Sonya said. "I enjoy movies and reading, too."

"Me too," Boone agreed. "I passed a library on the way here."

Sonya beamed. "I love libraries and can't wait to see what books they have."

"Maybe we'll stop by after we walk a bit."

Sonya glanced around. "Is this Paradise?

Boone took Sonya's hand, "Not until I met you."

The three aunts had hidden themselves behind some foliage and heard the exchange between Sonya and Boone. The two strolled into the garden, engrossed in conversation, both smiling.

The aunts emerged from their hiding place and continued to stare after the couple as they walked down the pathway toward the large three-tied fountain spurting water from stone angels

Aunt Bertie uttered, "That went well, don't you think, sisters?"

Aunt Betsy agreed, "Quite well, Bertie."

Aunt Beth Anne nodded her head.

The three were beaming as they stared after the couple.

Aunt Betsy said, "They look rather nice together, don't you think?"

"Yes, they really do," Aunt Bertie stated.

They caught a glimpse of Sonya and Boone at the fountain holding hands. The aunts grinned at each other and seemed quite pleased with themselves, and made their way through the park.

Aunt Beth Anne asked, "Do they know?"

"Oh no, not yet," Aunt Bertie replied.

"When will we tell them?" Aunt Betsy asked.

"We don't want to spring it on them too fast," Aunt Betsy said, smiling.

"So, when do we tell them?" asked Aunt Beth Anne.

"Let them get to know one another, first," said Aunt Bertie. "After all, time has little meaning here. Allow them a chance to find love and then, everything else will fall into place."

"Anyone for Bingo," asked Aunt Beth Anne.

The three hurried through the park, heading for the community center.

Aunt Betsy said, "I do hope Sheila saved us seats."

Aunt Bertie said, "Oh, I'm sure she did."

"Maybe after Sonya and Boone fall in love..." Aunt Beth Anne nodded to her sisters and crossed her fingers. "... they'll join us."

"Perhaps they might enjoy playing Bingo," Aunt Betsy said.

"Perhaps indeed," Aunt Bertie agreed, smiling broadly. "Let's see what happens afterwards."

FRUIT OF THE FAE

SCARLETT XAVIER

I found you in the garden, square-jawed and folded in shadow. You beckoned me to try your fruit, just like the serpent did in Paradise, but you were never anything so biblical. No, you were something more akin to the Fae.

In darkest Eden, you extended your hand. I took it, the electric pulse surging through me, igniting my heart.

"Give me your name. I'll keep it safe," you promised, your sapphire eyes gleaming in the dim light.

And I was foolish enough to believe it.

THE WINDS OF VALIHAR

JASMINE SIMPSON

The water that lapped against the shore was as black as tar, glinting wickedly in the harsh sunlight. Lady Atraine watched as the thick mass of it heaved forward and back, a dark stain across the white sands of Valihar.

"What devilry is beckoned forth?" Eron murmured beside her. His brows rested heavy over his hooded eyes as he stared out across the sickness. "This darkness does not bode well."

"I dare say it does not," she replied, her voice steady despite the unease stirring within her. She studied her father's face, recognizing the weight he bore across his shoulders. A king's burden, something neither she nor any other man could understand. These past few years, she had come to realize she did not know her father. Not as she once did. Since the death of her mother, he did not smile. His gaze held no warmth. As vile as his words could be at times, his frail body seemed to wither with each passing day.

"Come." She gently placed a hand over the crook of his arm, guiding him back towards the ramparts that kept the tides of the sea at bay. The crumbling walls of Valihar's fortress were strewn against the cliffside, almost as if it had fallen to earth from the heavens. Years of neglect and relentless war with Anator had all but ravaged her home. Were it not for the valiant efforts of her father's council and their strong-willed people, their home would have fallen long ago. All the same, a weariness dragged on in the heart of every man and woman. A grief, born from the loss of their queen.

"Speak with the council, Father. Summon them to Valihar. They must hear of this sickness."

She motioned him onward, only for a stray gust of wind to tug at the edge of her dress. It nipped at her hair and ghosted across her skin. Atraine stilled as the pull of it tempted her back to the sea.

"Atraine," the wind whispered a cold breath against her ears. Goosebumps stirred at the nape of her neck. It was a familiar presence, a voice that called to her many a time in the night. She looked back at the water, a strange, burgeoning sadness twisting inside her.

"Did you hear that, Father?" she breathed, closing her eyes as the wind continued to pull at her. "The winds are whispering. The sea is calling."

Eron scowled as he watched her, a shadow slipping over his face. "What good do empty tongues speak when a curse this very hour is placed upon us?"

Atraine opened her eyes once more and grasped his arm tighter, knowing all too well the blackness of his thoughts. She herself had drowned in it. When her mother died, there was no one to pull her from her sorrows. She would sit by the edge of the sea, once so blue and inviting, and think of her mother. She would cry for her, begging her to come back. She would curl into the sands and sleep, feeling nothing save the warmth of the sun and the kiss of the water as it threatened to pull her in.

It was not long before the voice without a name came to

her. The gentle caress of wind would hold her fast, soothing her sorrows with songs of the sea. She did not question it, nor did she speak of it to her father. She kept the voice to herself, a respite in the dead of winter when the touch of the sun had faded away.

Now, with summer at their heels, the black tide consumed all warmth. Cold and unfeeling. A harbinger of ill will for her and her people.

As she walked with Eron through the gates of the ramparts and into the courtyards, they passed the great hall and continued toward the keep where the garden spiraled. Atraine recalled an old saying of her mother's. One that she hoped would offer strength to her father in this time of uncertainty.

"By the work of reputable hands, many a rose shall bloom and grow," she quoted.

"Roses?" Eron hissed.

Atraine stepped back, startled at the sudden hostility in his eyes. Reaching out, he seized her by the hair and forced her gaze back upon her mother's garden. Atraine struggled, attempting to free herself from his iron grip.

"Look now, how this pallid gloom bends their filaments to the ground. These sickly sweet petals will wither and die, just as your mother did."

"Release me," she pleaded, her hands attempting to pry his fingers off her. He only gazed at her, his eyes becoming unfocused. He yanked her head to the side as he let go, leaving her to fall against the ground.

"You are not yourself. Surely you must see that." It took everything she had to not cry at the volatile changes in his moods. One moment, the doting father she had always known. The next, as if a stranger had taken hold of his mind.

Eron's body shook as he foamed at the mouth. He raised

his hand and backhanded her across the face. The pain of it lingered, leaving her with her head hung low, her hands clenching the dirt.

"A voice from the sea?" A mirthful laugh pealed from his lips. He grew frantic, letting his words carry across the open courtyard. "Fool!" he seethed. "That voice is not of the sea. It is a servant of hell that seeks the ruin of us all. You have brought it here, whispering to it in the shadows. Do not think that I do not know how it has seduced you, how it dragged your mother to her death."

"Oh, Father," she wept. "Would that I could drown in the sea if only to be free of this cruel sickness that plagues you."

Before he could grab hold of her again, she fled into the keep. As she climbed the stairs to her chambers, the stone walls hounded her at every turn, suffocating her. It was cold and damp, a ruin of a home that once held light. Even now, the meager flames guiding her way flickered with unease.

In her chambers, she paced for what felt like hours, her heart racing as the night approached quickly. Her lady's maid came and went, prodding her with food from the kitchens, preparing her for bed. Still, she could only watch the night sky through the narrow opening carved into the stone of her walls. She watched the clouds consume the last light of the moon and felt a sorrow settle deep into her heart. Like nothing she had ever felt before.

It was not long before rain pelted the walls of the keep, a raging storm flashing off the sea. She did not allow herself to wait any longer as a restlessness carried her out the door of her chambers. Her bare feet padding along the corridor, she raced to her father's rooms.

In a grip of deathly silence, she nudged open the door of his antechamber and crept across the hall into the main room. There on the armchair, beside his badly dented and rusting armor, lay her father's sword. As she reached out for it, a gentle breeze stirred at her wrists, staying her hand. The voice. It was here.

"Such darkness that finds you," the voice whispered. "Do you not fear it?"

"No," she replied, her hands firm as she grasped the sword. Lifting it soundlessly from its scabbard, she tightened her grip on the hilt and closed her eyes. A resolve had settled into her, guiding her through this night. "I only fear that which seeks to end me. The darkness merely veils it."

At that, the voice grew silent. Watchful.

She carried the weight of the sword through the shadows of the keep, down to the lower bailey and the flanking tower of the fortress that overlooked the cliffside. The wind coursed around her in a panic as she stared out into the ebony sea. Atraine let the pull of the water's presence drag her to the edge of the tower, till her feet nearly danced with the open air.

"Surely a man hath seen no more of grief than this," her father cried out behind her, "That even the sun should wane and tremble as a dying star."

She turned, resolve nearly faltering at the sight of him stumbling across the uneven stones to reach her. Even in his madness, even in his anger and reproach, he still looked to her. He still thought of her as the sun.

"Do you truly think I would fail you?" She could hardly bear to look at him as she asked the question she had dwelled on for the past several hours. "Do you think me a fool to try?"

"You would drown, as your mother did. You would lose yourself to the sea and never return."

By the heaving of his chest and the wind that tossed his hair back and forth, anyone might have thought he stirred with rage as before. But tears fell down his cheeks and his hands trembled. The same hands which had not held her safe in his arms for quite some time.

"I am stirred by the sentient sea," Atraine called out, shaking her head. "A commander that knows no restraints. A warrior of time. She will not abandon me yet." Upon the last breath of her words, she turned and plunged into the black sea. It was there that the light of the keep snuffed out and she was met only with the slick, heavy pull of the water. She sank down to the depths, her lungs now burning with a thirst for air.

Through the darkness, Atraine could discern that she was not alone. She sensed the writhing of a foul presence slithering beside her and thrust out her father's sword. The blade met nothing but the sea as she struggled to gain her bearings.

Something cold and piercing wrapped around her leg, a vice dragging her deeper through the water. She grabbed the hilt of the sword with both hands and plunged it into the body of darkness.

Loud wailing rippled through the water, black tongues lashing about. In the frenzy, her father's sword fell from her hands, and the final breath of air left her body.

A soft breeze tickled at the tips of her fingers. It trailed up the inside of her arm before lingering on her face. Her breath returned to her lungs, and she paused, gripping a fistful of the warm sand beneath her fingers.

A laugh that was not her own sounded against her chest, bright and unburdened. "Ah, here she lies, while in her threaded veil of sleep. Still as the grave, but quite well. My lady Atraine."

She knew that voice, she knew it so well that her eyes flung open and her heart hammered in disbelief. Blue eyes, as wild and uncharted as the sea, gazed into hers. He smiled, running a hand across her cheek, across her lips, reaching back to tangle fingers in her unruly hair. Though she did not know this face, she recognized the curiosity of his touch. The wind had so often embraced her just as he did now.

Tears fell from her eyes as she noticed the fresh wound across his chest. A wound made from her very blade. "You are my voice," she gasped.

"I am yours." He beamed at her only for a moment before crashing his lips over hers. And he kissed her as if all the air in the world were not enough. His hand at her back held her fast while the other moved from her hair to the curve of her neck.

All at once, Atraine pulled away. Her chest rose and fell as they looked at each other. A moment passed before she could draw another breath.

"You are wounded."

"Nothing but a scratch. It will heal."

"It was my fault," she cried.

He merely shrugged and held her gaze. "Had you not done so, I would not live this very moment before you."

At his words, all reason returned. She withdrew from his hold and stood, her eyes whipping to the ramparts, searching for her father.

It was the touch of Eron's hand on her shoulder, the feel of his arms as he finally pulled her toward him and held her close, that made a smile spread across her face. "My dear child," he murmured into her hair. "I am sorry."

Atraine could not find the words to express how relieved she was to have her father returned to her at last. She could only hold him tighter as the summer wind stirred about them.

Triggers: Discussion of Suicide

Jake, Allen, and Brett gathered by the front door of their frat house, dressed as ninjitsu-themed anthropomorphized adolescent turtle siblings.

"I'm telling you," said Jake, "we should have held a party here!"

"Yeah," agreed Brett, "nothing better than a true-life haunted Victorian house for the perfect Halloween rager."

"I'd grind on our hot resident ghost!" joked Jake, twirling his foam nunchucks into his own face.

"You'd have to ask Alex for permission," said Brett. "He's in love with Edwina the decapitated darling."

"Is that how she died? I thought it was poison or something," said Jake.

"There's no such thing as ghosts," observed Allen, checking his watch.

Brett swung his plastic swords wildly in the air. "Alex swears his room is haunted."

"I've heard him whispering at night," said Jake.

"At least if we hosted," said Brett, "we wouldn't have to worry about Alex making us late for the party..."

"The late, great Alex Cooper."

"Hey, Alex," called Allen, "We're gonna be late!"

Alex stepped out, dressed in Victorian-style garb from head to toe. "What do you think?" he said, spinning slowly in his ballroom regalia. He had a rope tied around his neck.

"What the hell, man? We're supposed to be a group costume!" said Allen.

"Oh my god, he's doing a couple's costume with his fake girlfriend!" Jake laughed.

The men busted out in laughter.

"OK, sorry, fellas. I'll *change* and meet you later."

"Fine, but hurry up." The three departed irritated.

Alex went to his room and hung himself from the rafters.

"Oh, Alex, you did it!" said a sweet, soft voice. It was the lovely Edwina, holding her head at her hips.

"Call me Alexander."

She blushed. "Yes, my dear Alexander."

"Shall we dance, my eternal beloved?"

Triggers: Sexual Content

Adrian watched Dawn's dainty fingers trace a simple arcane pattern in the space between them. Each sweeping motion of her hand added another luminescent petal to the spectral floral pattern taking shape in front of her. Magic rippled and shimmered around her. The gold that flecked her brown eyes had glowed. The faint olive undertone of her skin deepened until the entirety of her freckled skin shifted to a soft sage green as her glamor fell away.

A shiver ran down Adrian's spine; the once stuffy air of his apartment had turned electric. It prickled against his lithe body, a warm, half-forgotten sensation, like the faded memory of the sun against his living flesh. His mouth twitched up at the corner at Dawn's noble attempt to make the faerish language's melodic timber sound authoritative.

Dawn gave him a wicked smile before tightening the vines with a click of her fingers. Adrian let out a surprised grasp; his body lurched back, his head hitting the garden trellis that had once been his headboard with a soft thunk. A growl rumbled low in his chest, his upper lip curling back to flash the sharp points of his fangs, but Dawn only let out a peel of golden laughter.

"Oh, very funny," he said, suddenly realizing as the soft foliage tickled his skin that he was much more of a hand-talker than he'd been willing to admit. "You'll pay for that later."

Dawn tilted her head to the right, her loose hair falling over her shoulder, "Maybe I'll have to keep you like this forever, then?"

She took a step forward, leaning forward until her hands bracketed his shoulders. Her approach had been reasonably confident, but there was a flicker of uncertainty in her big brown eyes.

"You're sure you want to try this?" she asked.

Adrian pressed his forehead to hers, unable to fight off the besotted grin that had taken shape across his lips, "I'm sure, but thank you for asking."

She brought her hands behind her neck, tugging her negligee over her head. Adrian gave a weak attempt at silencing a low snicker as the fabric got caught on the long line of her ears in her haste. An adorable pink bloomed across the apples of her rounded cheeks. Her fingers returned to the satin ribbon at the front of her underwear once more, shimmying her wide, seductive hips as she slipped them off.

His breath caught in his chest as he drank her in. She was eternal. A goddess all his own. Plump curves. Full breasts. Her loose curls cascaded down her back like a river of rose petals. Freckles like flecks of gold covering her soft, kissable skin. She looked like a dream, dressed in nothing but her skin. He instinctively reached out to touch her, only to feel the vines around his wrist go taut, pulling him back to the headboard.

"My, my, someone is impatient!" she cooed, the mattress sinking slightly at the weight of her knee pressing into the space beside him. "You know, I've been thinking about something you said the other day. Can you really not see your own reflection?"

Adrian groaned, "I hardly see how the answer to that is relevant to the situation at hand, dear."

Unperturbed, Dawn simply gave him a sweet smile, moving painfully close to him before halting once more, "Humor me?"

"I really can't."

"So, you don't know what you look like?"

"I'm sure right now I look rather annoyed," he quipped back.

"I'm being serious."

Her lower lip jutted out ever so slightly. Her eyebrows stitched, and his heart threatened to melt into a puddle. He was certain she knew he'd cave if she gave him that look. He had been able to resist when they'd first met, but lately, that quivering lip was a sure-fire path to getting her way.

"Ugh- Alright! I'll indulge you! Little brat..." With a stroppy huff, he said, "I have a general idea of how I looked before. Lacking any evidence to the contrary, I just assume I look amazing."

"Dear me!" she touted with a chime of laughter, "So cocksure. You satisfied my curiosity." A coy smile flashed across her face, "For now, anyway. I think that deserves a reward."

"You are outstandingly beautiful, to confirm your suspicions," she hummed, straddling his hips.

He could feel her warm core against his length. He pressed himself against her, rocking slowly against her sex. She gave a delighted squeak, wiggling against the solid pressure of his erection. "I wish I could draw so you could see for yourself. Unfortunately, I'm hopeless with brush and canvas. I am quite good with gab, however. I could paint you a picture with words instead. Would you like that?"

He'd be lying if he claimed to have never been curious about his appearance. He had a few memories of his mortal countenance. But like most of his past, time and torment had left them hazy and abstract. He'd definitely had a little more color in life. He could recall being fair but not quite so cadaverously pale. His eyes would have been the most severe change, save the fangs. He'd seen the same haunting scarlet in the irises of every vampiric creature he'd met.

He flitted through his thoughts, trying to recall their previous color. Knowing Dawn, she'd eventually ask him, if not now, later on, one of her whimsical larks. He was somewhat sure they had been green. Her offer seemed more and more appealing as his mind shifted through faint, crumbing memories. It would be fascinating to hear what parts of him she'd taken particular notice of. Moreover, Dawn had the remarkable ability to see the absolute best in everything. His appearance would likely be much the same, and what man wouldn't want the object of his desire to spoil him with compliments?

"Go on," he affirmed with another eager roll of his hips against the growing wetness between her legs.

"Very well. You have a strong, angular jaw and perfect cheekbones. You have a little birthmark riiiiight Here!" Dawn noted the spot on his cheek with a peck, "You have the most heartbreakingly handsome grin I've ever seen. Your nose is very straight. I can tell you weren't in many bar fights!" She giggled, tapping the tip of his nose with her index finger.

Adrian scrunched his nose in response, prompting another musical laugh from Dawn. Followed by a long, slow kiss to his lips. He slid the edge of his tongue along the seam of her lips. A dissatisfied curse escaped him as she pulled back. Dawn only continued to beam with bemusement at his wanting. She brought a hand to a stray lock of hair that had fallen into his face. She wound the curl around her fingertip before sliding her fingers through his hair, tugging softly at the root as she pushed it back.

"Your hair is the color of moonlight. Your eyes are my favorite, though. So striking... The color of fine claret. Expressive too! If I want to know your mood, I can always see it in your eyes. Or by the tips of your ears. They go pink when you are flustered. It's faint, but I've spent enough time admiring you to notice." She nibbled his ear to emphasize her point, drawing a quiet whimper from Adrian. She kissed her way back down his body, pausing on the hollow of his neck and collarbones.

She slid off his hips, kidding each rib on the right side of his body before settling between his thighs. Her soft hand wrapped around his member. A needy growl fell from his lips as she began her lazy pumping. She let out a playful chime of laughter before running her tongue along the underside of his shaft.

"And, of course, your cock is glorious! So long with a slight curve that hits all my secret places. While I'm not the inexperienced maiden, you hilariously mistook me for, but you do make me feel as if I were. You make sex feel new and exciting, Adrian. You make my life exciting all around. Normally, my fancies come and go with haste, but I can't imagine ever growing bored with you. I've never had a lover hold my attention as you do."

Her adoring plaudits were overwhelming. Each comment was painfully sincere. Her free hand drifted between her legs. The licentious mewls she made as her fingers toyed with herself made him even harder. His mind was swimming with desire. He wanted nothing more than to plunge into her snug, wet sheath. She must have seen the hunger in his expression. His body went taut as he felt her soft lips around him. Gods, he wanted to touch her! To sink his fingers into her soft curls while she worshiped his cock. His hips bucked against her mouth as instinct took over. The sweet vibration of her giggles sent a shiver down his spine. He almost didn't notice the feeling of more plant life ensnaring him, ankle to the shin. He could feel himself swiftly approaching the brink as she teased his tip.

"Dawn..." His voice came out strained, "You'll need to stop soon. I'd still like to have you in other ways." With a hum of understanding, she removed him from her mouth with a soft pop. His wrist strained against his bindings as he attempted to reach for her hips. "Wait a moment. I want to taste you first."

"You want me to unbind you?" she asked.

"I didn't say that." He chuckled, a playful half-smile on his lips.

———

"Oh."

Dawn's belly flipped when she heard his request. The embers of confidence smothered by her insecurities. She'd had her fair share of lovers between her thighs, but she'd never like...That. Adrian was so lithe. She didn't want to smother him!

"You can say no, darling," he reassured, "However, if you are worried about hurting me, don't be."

Nibbling her lower lip, a hot flush broke out across her naked body. "How did you know?"

"It's a fairly common anxiety. I promise I'll be perfectly fine. Besides, if you accidentally suffocate me, you can just call that witch of yours and ask her if she'd be willing to dabble in a bit of necromancy."

Dawn tried to hold in her laughter, but it came out in a snort, "You are awful! What if she wanted to see your body?"

"Gods, I hope she would! Can you imagine her shock? Finding me all dressed up in jasmine after meeting my untimely end betwixt your gorgeous thighs!" he stated with a mirthful grin,

"This is all hypothetical, of course. I fully expect you'll be the only one to experience a little death from sitting on my face."

Dawn felt her nerves steadying with his gentle taunting. She couldn't decide if she was touched or mortified that he'd taken note of her insecurities. She'd never voiced them, but he had been perspective enough to notice the little changes in her demeanor. He had a knack for catching on to the little things other people tried to hide. Part of the wiles that had kept him alive for centuries. She supposed his perceptiveness was the flip side of his secrecy.

She brushed her lips against his. "Alright."

Dawn steeled herself as she settled her thighs on either side of him. Ever so slowly, she lowered herself towards his smirking mouth.

Oh wow.

All the worry slipped away with the first pass of his cool tongue along her slit. A lewd gasp broke free from her as he sealed his lips over her clit. Sucking and teasing her to delirium. Her hips grew a will of their own, rocking forward, chasing the electrifying sensation. Her squirming only seemed to encourage him. His attention shifted to the mouth of her arousal. His tongue eagerly explored her dripping center. Her confidence returned with each dizzying lick. She thought she'd feel ridiculous perched on top of him. The sight of Adrian happily ravaging her with his mouth left her feeling empowered and needy.

"Gods, that's good!" she whimpered, rutting against him, "I—wow... I kind of want to keep you here forever."She tugged at the roots of his soft curls, pulling him deeper into her arousal. Promoting a delighted purr from Adrian as he continued to lap away at her quim. "Keep going! I'm so close... Ah! Adrian! Please! More!" A few more skillful sweeps of his tongue and the hot coil of building pleasure snapped loose.

She hadn't meant for the lamentation that followed to come out at such a high volume. She usually tried to be courteous to the neighbors. The walls of his apartment were thin, and they would likely not enjoy her keening half as much as Adrian did. She bit down her lip, quieting another cry as the tempest of exaltation mixed with the sharp sensation of his teeth on her inner thigh. After a few swallows, he brushed his lips over the wound in a chaste kiss. She climbed down from her seat, flopping down on his chest. Her breath came out in ragged heaves.

"That was life-changing."

She glanced up, finding him staring with even more hunger than usual. His chin shimmered with slick, his lips stained red by her blood, and his eyes alighted with impatient longing.

"Years of practice," he stated with a wicked grin. "Now if you'd be kind enough to free me? If I don't have my way with you this instant, I might be driven mad."

She nodded, climbing off his chest to receive one of his daggers from his things. She carefully cut away the blossoms and vines that held him prone. As soon as the blade cleared the twist of greenery, he pounced, laying her out on her stomach. Dawn let out a peal of amusement, propping herself up slightly on her elbows. Adrian ran his finger along her slit, causing her to shiver. A dark, desirous sound rumbled in his chest as he sunk two fingers into her.

"Still a little sensitive, are we? There is still nectar dripping from your flower down the back of your legs. I knew you'd enjoy your little ride. I certainly did. You're so beautiful when you come undone. Squirming and squealing. I wonder what the others will say now that they've heard you screaming my name like a trollop?" He let out a moan as Dawn clenched around his pumping fingers, "Should we see if I can get you to do it again?"

Dawn cried out as he impaled her with one urgent push. His hips met hers with a smack before he withdrew almost completely. She whined at the emptiness, relief washing over her as he resheathed himself with another unyielding shove. It seemed to be unable to touch her had inspired a carnal frustration he was desperate to satisfy. He gathered her loose hair up in one hand, yanking her back as he continued to pound into her. He hissed as Dawn brought her thighs closer together, savoring the hardness of his length inside her.

"Tell me again, tart," he demanded, wrenching her back to look at him, "Tell me how I make you feel like a vestal maid with my 'glorious cock'."

"For you, I am reduced to an untouched damsel," she confirmed, pushing her backside against him.

"Indeed you are." He released his grip on her curls, bringing his hands to rest on the swell of her hip, tugging her even closer.

He growled his approval before sinking his teeth into the warm hollow of her throat. With each sip, she felt his heart fall into step with her own. It was a strange sort of intimacy that felt a bit metaphorical. Cold and wicked, Adrian's undead heart lurched to life, beating in perfect time with her own as she coursed through him. Dawn knew it was a silly, romantic notion, but that could hardly be helped, especially when he was ravaging her with such vigor. Her second climax flourished as he pressed himself against her just so. She convulses under him, tears streaming down her cheeks. Adrian tore himself away from her neck, incarnadine eyes burning ravenous with a mix of thirst and fearsome wanton need.

———

He shouldn't have bitten her again. It was a rash, risky choice, especially when he was already frenzied with lust. That first taste from her thigh had been the most exquisite yet. The sweetness of her blood mingling with the earthy tang of her slick had been transcendent. The soft, sunny joy he'd experienced when feeding on her in the past had been replaced with a blinding exaltation that had nearly finished him off untouched. It took no small amount of willpower to chase off his instinct to drink her dry.

As he beheld her writhing, buxom from an admission rushed out of him, "I never want anyone else to touch you again."

"I'm spoiled for all others. No one else could please me as you do."

Her words ignited something base in him, pushing him to the edge. With a final crude thrust, he found his rapture, flooding her snug, soaking heat with his release. All the while, his thoughts rang loudly with one word.

Mine.

COME ON BABY, LIGHT MY FIRE
KEYRA K. ALLRED

"Oy, watch it!" Annika grunted, backing away from the torch that almost lit her up like a solstice bonfire. The person who bumped into her turned, an apology on their lips, and Annika was mortified to discover the cloaked figure was Eva.

"I'm so sorry, Annika," the young woman said, "are you alright?"

Ignoring the bit of char on her shoulder, Annika mumbled, "It's fine. No worse for wear."

Eva would not be swayed. She noticed the blackened edge of Annika's cape, her hand flying to her mouth, horrified. "No! Look what I've gone and done! Ugh! I'm such a clumsy fool!"

"I-No-It really is fine, Eva," Annika stuttered, wishing for the earth to open under her for the chance to get away from her mushy brain and bumbling mouth. She deeply hoped that the flames surrounding them hid the flaming in her cheeks. The forlorn expression on Eva's incomparably beautiful face was doing the exact opposite to Annika's emotions than she needed in this moment.

Those doe eyes staring out at her from above pleasantly

plump cheeks always showing off a kind smile did things to Annika that she couldn't explain.

Eva placed a gentle hand to her shoulder, the one not bearing a deep singe mark. "I shall fix it!" Eva said, determinedly before her face fell as another thought entered her mind. "Though I do not know how. I've never been one for the sewing arts."

Annika stumbled. It was well known that Eva was good at everything. The entire village sang her praises as often as two or more people found themselves together.

Annika's disbelief must have shown because Eva giggled, even as the crush of people slowly moved. "Oh, I know. Everyone thinks I'm so talented, but it isn't true. My parents just say all sorts of ridiculous things, and now who knows the truth of it all?"

Annika gaped. This was all news to her.

"Well, the truth is that I am deficient in many aspects of lady-like behavior and sewing is my worst subject. But," she continued, "I shall find a way to mend your cape so that it is better than new. I promise."

Eva held out her hand to shake on their pact, one which Annika had yet to gather her wits to understand. Switching the sickle to the hand holding the torch, which nearly had her awkwardly setting herself alight, Annika freed her right hand to nervously take Eva's. However, the other girl stared, transfixed, at the tool.

"Oh, that's lovely!" cried Eva, captivated.

Annika hesitated, feelings clogging her throat like leaves damming a stream. "Um, thanks."

"Did Dominik make this?" Eva reached out her free hand to touch the flat of the dark blade.

"No, he, uh, didn't," Annika replied, before whispering, " I did."

"*You* did?" Eva's voice was loud, but instead of being incredulous in an offensive manner, she sounded awestruck. Annika shouldn't be surprised. Her brother was the village blacksmith, not her.

It wouldn't have occurred to most of these people that she had learned many things alongside him and that he often allowed her to try her hand at a few pieces under his watchful eye. He was a good brother like that, and somewhere near the front of the throng, she guessed.

"Yes?" Annika replied, hesitantly. No one else in the village knew or cared about much of anything she did.

Eva evidently thought differently. "This is phenomenal work, Annika. May I?"

Annika handed the sickle to the woman who held it as though it were the very Spear of Longinus which pierced the side of the Christ. Annika was proud of it, the tool had taken her quite awhile to get just right, but the reverence shown by Eva swelled in a sort of exhilarated satisfaction.

Eva turned the sickle this way and that, running her eyes over the hammered metal. "You really have a gift. I am so proud of you and also a little jealous," Eva said, throwing Annika a quick wink. If not for the crush of bodies, Annika might have tripped over her skirts. As it was, the breath left her and she nodded shakily in thanks.

"What else have you made?"

"I—" Nobody paid much attention to Annika because she was a girl and definitely the least talented of her siblings. Her sister, Gretchen could cook so as to make the blind see, not to be blasphemous about it. "Mostly, Dominik has me make nails for him. He says they take too much time when he could be making things more suited to his gifts, but I've repaired some gardening tools." Annika suddenly remembered one project she had been particularly proud of. "I made a set of new spoons for mama's name-day. I got to learn how to add some pretty filigree to them."

"That's wonderful! I should very much like to see them."

Annika stumbled, shyly, "They weren't much, but mama said she loved them."

"I am sure they are perfectly beautiful. If this is anything to go by, they are good enough to serve the Emperor himself." Eva flashed her a wide grin and Annika was left speechless. Eva shivered, handing back Annika's tool to clutch at her fine cloak. "I am glad it is only a little chilly tonight, otherwise I might be much more miserable."

Annika hunted around her waist, trying not to hurt herself while she sought out a spare pair of mittens. She had none and glanced at Eva, crestfallen.

"No, no. Do not trouble yourself. I shall be just fine." Eva's eyes glinted with mischief. "I suppose we shall have to stay very close together to ward off the night air, yes?"

She leaned heavily toward Annika, bumping their shoulders. Annika froze, then, slowly, allowed herself to melt into the other woman's warmth. Several minutes passed, Annika deep in wonderment before an idea popped into her head.

"I have—umm—here." Annika carefully removed one of her own mittens and jerkily thrust it out for Eva to take.

"Oh, my. You don't have—"

"Now we can both be warm," Annika said with a shy smile.

Eva studied her a moment, then nodded, eagerly pushing the rough wool over her soft hand. Turning her head, Eva whispered, "Thank you for sharing your warmth with me, Annika."

The two women, happier now, trudged their way among the mob of villagers winding up the slippery mountain path to Castle Frankenstein.

Zane

How long has it been?

Since I last saw you?

Since you smiled and laughed beside me?

Your warmth is still entwined with mine as we lay in bed, not wanting to get up yet...

The smell of fresh grass and sunflowers—that's how I first met you.

You always loved sunflowers, always wore something to represent them.

Why did you have to leave me?

You didn't have to go so soon.

You didn't have to leave me alone.

It has been four years since Scarlet passed. I'm still living in the same town, the same part of it, but in a different house. I couldn't stay there after losing her. I could feel the emptiness in every room and couldn't handle it. I miss her so much.

People say I should move on, but I can't. She was the love of my life. You don't just get over losing that. It can take years to heal, and I feel like people forget that sometimes. No matter how much pain someone carries, others often don't listen.

"Zane! Look! The cherry blossoms have already bloomed!" you shouted the moment I stepped outside.

Your smile was so bright, so full of joy. You always wanted me to be the first to see our tree bloom each year.

"Scarlet, you're shouting," I teased as I came beside you.

Your face flushed. You covered your mouth, embarrassed.

Spring is nearly here again. My first one without you. I consider cutting the cherry tree down. I almost did. But something always holds me back—like you are telling me not to.

Odd, but... I listen.

This morning, as I step outside, I notice the warmth. The news said it would still be cold today. They are wrong—again.

I headed off to work.

Scarlet

I watch you from the doorway, concern heavy in my heart. Of course, you note the weather, surprised by the unexpected warmth.

You haven't gone out much lately. Not unless it was for work. Barely answering calls or texts. My loss hit you harder than I ever expected. What could I do? How could I help you move forward? I just want you to be happy—even without me.

I follow you to the college library—you always loved working there. You're quiet, but you love helping those who need it. It's one of my favorite things about you.

You clock in and get to work. I scan the room. Only a few students were scattered about. One caught my eye. Around your age. Shoulder-length black hair, dark green eyes. Casual clothes: black T-shirt, dark blue hoodie, jeans. Fingernails painted the same shade as his hoodie. Double-pierced ears.

He feels different. There's a warmth around him. A light. I'm drawn to him, and maybe you could be, too.

I return to your side, sorting through ideas as you put our favorite romantsy series back on the shelf—Hearts and Glass —back on the shelves.

I know exactly what I need to do.

Zane

I grab a stack of seven books, but as I do so something snags on my shirt, causing me to drop the books.

I curse, kneeling down to pick them up.

"Are you alright?"

Meeting the gaze of a very attractive stranger, I stare open-mouthed. I've seen him around, but always distracted, and always very far from me. But now he's right here—his legs inches from my face.

"Oh, yeah. I think my shirt got caught on the bookshelf," I reply, standing up. He's taller than me by several inches, so my eyes keep dropping to his lips and those perfectly white teeth of his.

"As long as you're okay," he says, grabbing the fallen books and setting them on the bookshelf—not in the right place, but close enough. "You are always here. I hope you aren't working too hard."

The comment caught me off guard. "Oh, I... I just work a lot."

His gaze was questioning after I answered, but he then gave a small smile.

"Well, don't work too hard. You don't want to burn yourself out. My name's Luca."

"Zane," I say, trying to fight the mixture of euphoria and guilt. I want to be happy about this guy, but it also feels like a disservice to Scarlet. "Well, I'll see you around?"

It looks like he wants to say something, but then he just nods and turns away. My heart thumping hard in my chest as I see him retreat back to his seat. I haven't felt like this since...

Well, since I met Scarlet.

Scarlet

Don't feel guilty—seriously. This is exactly what I want for you. I repeat the phrase over and over until I think it gets through to you, but by then you've already watched Luca leave, and you're left overworking, like you always do.

But I can feel your heart. I feel how excited you are, and over the next few days, I feel that guilt wash away. And eventually, you actually believe you deserve this—that I would be happy for you.

Because I would, and I am.

You even give him your number, and you let yourself laugh. It's good to hear your laugh again. I almost forgot you knew how to do it.

Zane

Luca asked me on a date.

I was shocked at first. I had never dated another guy before, but... I love being around him and spending time with him. It feels familiar... like with Scarlet.

So I went with him to the park. He was by the pond, photographing playful swans. I didn't want to interrupt. But he noticed me.

"You're early," he says with a soft smile.

"Better than being late, right?" I joke.

He laughs. Such a soft, beautiful sound.

A breeze passed us, carrying cherry blossoms through the air. And I hear your voice, "You'll be fine."

"Zane? You okay?"

"Huh? Sorry. I heard someone."

"Well, I was talking about the giant steak I'm going to buy you for lunch. You're going to be crawling out of the restaurant when we're through."

I smile. "Yes, it must be that." But in my head, I whisper, "Thank you, Scarlet."

And she whispers back, "We will be fine. I will be fine. You don't have to worry about me again."

THE FRAT BOY GHOST WHO HAUNTED MY HOUSE

SARA FITZGERALD

Katherine

Katherine trudged up the creaky stairs, shivering and fumbling with her keys. The porch light flickered under the October moon. A black cat hissed and scurried off the sagging porch, as if warning her of something hidden inside the old house.

Her phone buzzed. She rolled her eyes. Her mom—again.

She opened the door and shut it behind her. "Hey, mom."

Katherine kicked off her shoes and dropped her backpack onto a dusty chair. The place smelled strange, but the rent was cheap and the house came furnished.

"I'm fine," she muttered, heading to the bedroom. "I'm not working too hard."

She swallowed her frustration. Her parents wanted her to be independent, yet hovered like helicopters.

"I know you're not thrilled I'm living next to the Salt Lake Cemetery, but it's quiet. Not haunted!" she added with a forced chuckle. "I'll call you tomorrow. Love you."

Her last living quarters had six other roommates who thought college was about frat boys, booze, and parties. Thank goodness she found this nice place. She crawled into bed, tugging the blankets up tight. The house was almost as cold as outside. The creaking was unsettling, but it was an old house. It was to be expected.

Brent

Brent's lips twitched with amusement as he gazed at the sleeping girl. How long would she last?

She didn't seem the type to enjoy hard rock. More like classical music and cramming for finals. Poor thing looked exhausted. He'd let her sleep tonight, but tomorrow? All bets were off.

He sighed. It wasn't his fault she moved in. Why should he be forced to suffer in silence? He died during the best years of his life—and got stuck here.

His dad had been right: the band never made it out of the garage. What were his friends doing now? Still jamming?

Katherine

Katherine slammed the front door. Her body ached; her brain was fried. Flyers for frat parties littered the campus, but no one invited her. She didn't care. Beer was disgusting, and frat boys worse. College should be about learning.

Loud 80s music blared. She jumped. What the hell? Had someone broken in? Where was

the music coming from? It was like a freaking rock concert from a time machine.

She picked up a heavy textbook. "Who's here?"

"*Chill*," said a smooth male voice.

She spun around, textbook raised.

"Gonna hit me, or just bore me to death with that?" he asked, stepping into the light.

He was shirtless, in faded jeans, and infuriatingly gorgeous.

"Is this a prank?" she snapped. "Get out—or I'll report you."

He shrugged. "Been tiptoeing all week. But it's Friday. Time to party like a normal college kid."

"All week?" Her stomach dropped. "Have you been... here... the whole time?"

Fear prickled up her spine. Had he been living in her walls this whole time, like some creep out of a Lifetime movie?

"I'm calling the police," she snapped, grabbing her phone.

"Whoa, chill." He held up his hands. "I think we got off on the wrong foot. There's no easy way to say this, so... yeah, I live here."

Her fingers fumbled as she dug out her pepper spray. "Stay back! I'm warning you—I'll use this."

"I'm sorry—"

She didn't wait for an explanation. She pressed the button, but nothing happened. He was standing in the mist, but he was perfectly okay. Why wasn't the pepper spray working?

"I see this is a lot to process," he said, rocking back on his heels. "But maybe you should, like, break your lease. I don't think we're cut out to be roommates. No hard feelings."

She stared at him, stunned.

"Although..." He smirked. "You're kind of sexy. Could be fun having someone around again."

"Excuse me?"

He shrugged like he hadn't just crossed every line imaginable. "The last tenant was this old lady with, like, a hundred cats. You can still smell them if you try. She died here, by the way.

Thank God she crossed over. Can't imagine being stuck with her forever."

"You're a ghost? Prove it," she said.

"What?"

"You heard me. You can't expect people to believe you are supernatural just because you

say so." She crossed her arms. "Go ahead."

"You just sprayed me with pepper spray and nothing."

"Look, first off, you still haven't proven a thing; second, my name is Katherine; third, I'm not so sure I like you; fourth, your taste in music is questionable; and fifth, this is my home."

He disappeared and reappeared.

"Do you want to wave your hand through me?" he said, walking to her, standing inches away.

She swallowed hard. He was sexy, dead, and her new roommate. *God help me.*

Katherine

Katherine's stomach tightened as she stared at the house. A month had passed, and still, the ghost unsettled her more than she wanted to admit. The feelings scared her—not just because he was dead, but because she couldn't stop thinking about him.

And nothing could ever come of it. Obviously.

They couldn't even touch.

Her grandma once claimed that if two souls truly intertwined, their bodies could merge. Katherine rolled her eyes just remembering it. That would never happen. He was a frat boy from the '80s, for goodness' sake. Eventually, she'd fall for someone with a pulse—or adopt a dozen cats and live happily ever after among the litter boxes.

She pushed open the front door, and the cold seeped into her bones. The furnace still didn't work right—because of him.

Brent sat on the couch, one leg crossed over the other, brow furrowed.

"You're late," he said. Then he shrugged like it didn't matter. "Not that I was waiting or anything."

"Sorry, classes ran late. But I brought pizza." She held out the box. "Your favorite."

"Bitchin'." He jumped off the couch, inhaling deeply. "God, you're perfect."

She laughed. "It's just pizza." She set the box on the table. "Want to finish our show?"

"What about studying?"

"It can wait—just for tonight." She'd never blown off a night of studying to watch Battle of the Bands, but she'd also never had a ghost roommate. *Life was full of surprises.*

"You know, my band could have gotten on Battle of the Bands if I hadn't died." There was a heaviness in his words, and even though he couldn't pick up the pizza, he still picked at the air around it like he still could grab bits of cheese.

"You never told me how you died."

He looked away. "Does it matter?"

"It does to me."

A shadow crossed his features. "Party. I mixed stuff—drugs, alcohol. That was it. One night and... gone."

"I'm sorry."

"Me too. It was a bogus way to die."

She reached for his hand and, to her shock, felt something. A spark, real and electric, flicked through the air.

Katherine sat frozen, her hand still tingling from the spark.

It wasn't her imagination. She'd felt him.

He stood up abruptly. "It's late. You should sleep."

"No, wait—"

But he had already disappeared down the hall.

She glanced down at her fingers, half-expecting them to glow or twitch or vanish into mist. But they were just fingers—warm, trembling, alive.

Had her grandma really been right? Could their souls really intertwine? That seemed silly, but it was still enough to give her the momentum to move from her spot.

The house creaked around her—its usual ghostly protest—but tonight, it felt different. She found Brent in the spare bedroom. He stood near the window, his silhouette lit by the streetlamp outside.

"Hey," she said softly.

He didn't turn around. "You shouldn't have felt that."

"Why not?"

"Because I'm not real, Katherine. I'm just... echoes. Memories. I'm not supposed to touch anyone. That's not how this works."

She stepped closer. "But you did."

He exhaled shakily. "So what? We merge into some ghost-human hybrid? I haunt you forever while you try to go on dates and explain why you can't move on because your undead boyfriend keeps vacuuming your place?"

She smiled despite herself. "Honestly, that sounds more helpful than most of the guys I've dated."

He finally looked at her, eyes heavy with something unspoken. Regret? Longing?

"I don't want to be the thing that keeps you from living."

She walked up to him, closing the distance. "You're not. You make me feel things again. Things I thought were dead."

Brent stared at her like she was breaking every rule he'd clung to for the past forty years. "Katherine..."

She reached out again, slowly, daringly, and touched his hand.

This time, it didn't spark.

It held.

Warmth bloomed between their palms, his fingers curling around hers as if they were no longer separate. He looked down, eyes wide.

"I feel you," he whispered.

"I feel you, too."

Twenty Years Later — Katherine

Katherine walked into their home. Her head pounded with another massive headache. She glanced in the mirror. More gray hair. It was probably from all the stress of running her community center. Brent at least always found a way to cheer her up.

Brent sauntered into the living room. "Hey, Babe. I missed you. Why so late?"

She slipped off her high heels and embraced her Frat Boy Ghost "All the red tape with the non-profits. Sometimes I think I should just—"

He frowned. "What?"

"Give up. I'm tired." Her shoulders sagged in defeat. "It shouldn't be this hard."

His hands danced down her back. "You know what I would say."

"If you were alive, you'd still be jamming no matter how hard it was, and to cherish my life while I have it."

"That's my girl."

He squeezed her close.

Her heart bounced with a mixture of love, desire, and

longing. The pounding in her head subsided. "How did you get so wise for a college boy?"

"Some beautiful young woman walked through that door and made me realize not to take a single moment for granted."

She arched her eyebrow. "She's lucky to have stolen your heart."

"Who says anything about my heart?" Laughter cavorted in his eyes. "She just lets me live here rent-free and gets me pizza anytime I want."

She smiled. "You can't even eat the pizza!"

"It's the thought that counts."

She laughed. "Sure."

"One more thing, your mom called and left a message about some nice chiropractor who just got divorced."

She pulled back. "Oh bother, she never gives up, does she?"

"Can you blame her? She doesn't want you to die alone." He smiled at her with amusement. "And she wants grand-kids. Your eggs are almost rotten. Her words, not mine."

"Lovely. Wish I could tell her about you."

"Then she'd be tripping about you."

They laughed. She ordered pizza. He cranked up the music, and they danced like college kids having the time of their lives.

Fifty Years Later — Katherine

Katherine lay in bed in her colorful living room, sun shining through the large bay windows. Her cats curled beside her, except Mangy, who was chewing her loveseat. She felt a potent mixture of love, sadness, and gratitude. Her life had been a good one; she couldn't complain. It had been filled with a sense of purpose, good friends, many cats, and most of all, the ghost she loved.

"I'll see you bright and early," said the young hospice worker.

"Take your time, dear." Katherine squeezed her hand. "No hurry."

"You have everything you need?"

She barely nodded. "I'm fine. Just lock the door on the way out."

"Is there someone you want me to call to be with you?"

"I've said my goodbyes." Except to her Frat Boy.

The young lady left. Brent crawled into the hospital bed with her. She curled up next to him. He stroked her thin, white hair, tears in his eyes.

"What's wrong, darling?" she asked.

"I'm going to miss you," he whispered.

"What?"

"You'll move on to somewhere beautiful." His lips brushed hers. "I'm happy for you. I just wish I could go with you."

"I'll never leave you or our cats."

He chuckled. "You are strongheaded as ever, but you won't get your way this time. You've lived a good life and changed lives for the better."

She struggled to take her next breath. What if he was right? She couldn't bear the thought of eternity without her ghost, not to mention the smell of pizza and rocking out to their 80s music.

"I love you, Kat."

"I love you."

She gasped. Life was draining out of her—just a few more breaths. A sob caught deep inside her. She wanted to say so much more. He changed her life, made it fun and full of love and music. Not to mention, he had always been so support-ive. She'd never have had the guts to open the community center if he hadn't believed in her.

"It's going to be okay." He held her tight. "You'll see a light. Just relax into it."

She took her last breath.

An explosion of brightness illuminated the room. She heard her parents, calling for her. Her soul drifted upward in a deep trance fading into the light.

Brent's head hung in despair. His beautiful Katherine was gone forever, and he was stuck here. She had made sure he and the cats would be well cared for, but eternity without her was too much to bear.

Noise thundered through the house. The cats jumped off the bed, backs arched and wildly hissing. The lights flickered, and a cold rush of air swirled through the living room.

His head jerked upward.

"Katherine, don't you dare go back there!" a woman screamed.

"Sorry, mom," she said, crashing through the ceiling.

She fell hard onto the hospital bed, smashing it to the floor. His eyes met hers, and a delicious grin fell upon his face.

"You always did manage to get your way," he said.

"I couldn't let you have all the fun. We have art classes, and to finish reading all the books we've been collecting. Not to mention we need to finish our murder podcast. Plus, you finally got an Xbox with every game possible."

"Not only that, but we also have plenty of time for this." He leaned down and devoured her lips with a passionate kiss.

Her toes tingled and happiness settled right inside her. She did get her way, Brent was right, she always did.

———

A young girl and her mom walked by the old home. The lights flickered, and 80s music drifted into the evening. Stray cats climbed the porch, hoping to find a home.

"Who lives there, mommy?" The girl pointed to the well-cared-for house.

Her mom squeezed her tiny hand. "Well, a nice old lady did for a long time, but since she died, no one has."

The girl's eyes grew wide. "But—"

"I think it's haunted," her mom said as a Pizza Hut car drove into the driveway.

"Do ghosts eat?" the girl asked with a puzzled face.

Her mom shrugged. "I have no idea, kiddo. Come on, let's head home and order our own pizza."

The girl grinned, glancing back once more as the ghosts' laughter filled the midnight sky.

SO I DATED A VAMPIRE

MAE THORN

"Are you all right?" the tattoo artist asked.

Hayley hissed in a breath. "I'm fine." She plastered on a false smile. *She would not faint.*

The tattoo artist shook her head and carved black butterfly wings into her upper arm. *This was nothing,* Hayley thought. Last week she had her nipples pierced. Now, *that* hurt. She could do this.

It was one more act of defiance, one more dose of freedom. She'd turned eighteen a month ago, and all she could think of was getting away, but self-mutilation would have to suffice.

Hayley braced her arm and thought of anything but the pain. The stabbing sensation stung as the butterfly came to life. Its wings exhibited a shadow that made the insect appear in flight.

"It's beautiful."

The tattoo artist cracked a smile. "Almost done." She worked in a circular motion, capturing the deep blue on the wings. "Careful. Drink some water and get something to eat." She handed Hayley a slip of paper. "Follow these instructions. Keep the second skin on for about a week. It helps prevent infection."

"Great." Hayley steadied herself against the counter while she studied the clear wrapping on her new tattoo. She handed the artist a wad of cash.

The sun tilted on the horizon, bringing fresh shadows to the street. Hayley popped her keys into the driver-side door and launched herself onto the seat of the car, just as her phone vibrated on the center console. She rolled her eyes. It was her friend, Gretchen.

"Hi, darling. Are you going to the party tonight? The one at Club 41?" She paused. When Hayley didn't answer, Gretchen said. "You did get my invite, didn't you?"

Gretchen was always sharing Facebook events. Hayley couldn't keep any of them straight.

"I don't know if I can make it. I just got a tattoo, and I'm not feeling great."

"You *what?* Listen, meet me in two hours. I know the bouncer, and he'll let us in. Wear something skanky."

"Fine, but if I pass out it's on your head."

Hayley eyed herself in the rearview mirror. Her green eyes looked back at her. She stuck out her tongue and started the car. She ripped off the second skin, not caring about the instructions. She didn't want the bandage like thing obstructing her view of the tattoo. It was well over two hours later when Gretchen pulled into Club 41.

Hayley tapped her foot as her friend drove up. "You're late."

Gretchen handed her keys off to the valet and strutted over to Haylee with open arms. "You look stunning."

Hayley had on a flowy blue skirt and matching halter top that barely held her breasts in. Gretchen wore a bright yellow dress and hoop earrings, making her bronze skin glow.

The music hit them first. The base pumped out like the beating of Hayley's heart, and a goofy grin touched her lips.

"Let's get a drink." Gretchen pulled Hayley to the bar.

"Impatient, are we?"

Gretchen waved a hand at the bartender. "Tom Collins."

Hayley frowned. "That's pure sugar."

Gretchen narrowed her eyes. "Bite your tongue."

"She can bite mine." A deep-throated voice penetrated through the music.

Hayley spun around and raised a finger at the arrogant man's chest, *and holy hell what a chest!* He was dark. Yeah, the tall, dark, and handsome type that girls *go gaga* for. Something about him said *danger*. Maybe it was that spicy aroma that was making her mouth water, or maybe it was the plump deep pink of his lips that cried for attention. He had a magnetism about him that made her want to crawl toward him.

"Charming," she said.

He grasped her finger and kissed her hand. "Enchanting."

At some point, Gretchen had vanished, leaving her with the towering, trouble of a man. She took a sip of a drink she didn't remember ordering. Chocolate martini, her favorite.

He chuckled. "Delicious. Just like you, Hayley."

Her insides did a flip. "What did you say your name was?"

"Stephen."

"Well, Stephen, let's dance." He tugged her onto the dance floor.

The music drummed through her. She didn't recognize the artist, but the lyrics slid from her lips like an old favorite. She ground her hips, and Stephen's breath teased her neck. A fire ignited inside her. He trailed his lips over her neck and touched her butterfly. She winced but let him kiss the ink. He ran his tongue over the surface. "It's bleeding."

She shivered, but the wound on her arm had stopped hurting though the little butterfly legs tingled.

He nibbled on her lower lip.

He was the man she desired. The man she had waited for her whole life. The man who was now pulling her into a dark corner.

"I've waited years to find you, Hayley."

She blinked. *Years? How is that possible?* She couldn't help but think he knew just what to say to entice a girl. She had read enough fated mate romantasy to fall for it.

His mouth went to her neck and two pinpricks penetrated her skin. A trickle of blood slid down her neck, but Hayley barely noticed. Wave after wave of warmth left her in a pool of ecstasy.

Stephen lapped at the blood he hadn't sucked dry. He smoothed a hand on Hayley's back, and she groaned.

The warmth settled low in her belly, melting her in Stephen's arms.

He kissed the two pinpricks and chuckled. "Better?"

"Yes," she croaked. She panted, an unbearable longing clawed at her. "Take me home." She grasped onto his tie and met his eyes. The black of his pupil seemed to grow as she watched. "I'm yours."

Stephen held up his hands. "Excuse me for a moment while I use the restroom." He touched a hand to his chest. "It's been a pleasure."

Her smile grew to goofy proportions as he walked away. She waited in a nearby booth, her head in her hands as she lay curled around the seat. She startled at the sound of Gretchen's voice.

"Time to go." Gretchen grabbed Hayley by the ankles and pulled her to the floor.

"Where is Stephen?"

"Your goth daddy?" Gretchen frowned. "He left hours ago with some other lady."

Hayley's heart sank, but before she could say anything, Hayley had ushered outside and into the passenger side of her car.

They rode in silence until Gretchen broke the peace.

"You shouldn't let vampires take advantage of you."

"Vampires?" Hayley was wide awake now. Her stomach twisted in knots. He had used her. Used her like cattle and hadn't even bothered to sleep with her.

"Especially the vampire *men*."

"As opposed to vampire women?" She laughed.

Gretchen stared straight ahead. "Mmm-hmm."

"Gretchen, are you sure you should be driving? What drugs are you on?"

Gretchen shook her head and pulled over. "I'm not on drugs."

A flash of pain in Hayley's neck reminded her of his teeth, his embrace, his darkness. "Whoa."

Gretchen held her hand. "I suspected. I'm sorry."

Hayley's brows knit together. "What's next? Werewolves?"

"Well..."

"How could you know he was a vampire?"

Gretchen fell into silence. "Because I am one."

Hayley coughed out a laugh. "No, you aren't."

"Have you ever seen me out during the day?"

"No, but you work."

"From home in the dark."

Hayley studied Gretchen. She was the same friend, the

same beautiful woman that Hayley had known for years. Gretchen smiled at her, emphasizing her fangs.

"Oh my God. You're a vampire!" Hayley reached out to touch Gretchen's fangs.

"You're not freaked out?"

"Of course not. If you were going to kill me, you would have done it ages ago. I kind of like it."

Gretchen let out a long breath. "There is another thing."

"What?"

"This." Gretchen leaned into Hayley, taking her lips with hers. Hayley flinched at first because she had never been with a woman before. She returned the kiss, and a buzzing heat spread over Hayley's body.

"Wow."

"Yeah."

"Can we do that again?"

Gretchen chuckled. "We can kiss all night if you want."

"I'd like that."

Gretchen pecked Hayley. "Let's get you home."

Triggers: Discussion of Suicide

Moving here was supposed to be a fresh start, but the peeling yellow wallpaper and creaky floorboards made it feel like the past had followed Melissa.

Placing the dish soap under the sink, she heard the crackle of the old 1960s kitchen radio as it sprang to life.

"Officials are still investigating the mysterious disappearance of Derek Hughes," a broadcast began.

The air around her grew heavy and cold, sending a flood of chills down her spine.

"Oh, Derek, not today!" she groaned.

She frantically fiddled with the old radio, but the knobs wouldn't budge. Her fingers ached as she tugged harder, but the broadcast grew louder: "his wife is no longer a suspect."

With a frustrated sigh, she let go and stumbled outside to find Corbin carrying the last load of boxes from the truck. He was Derek's business partner in their floundering maple syrup business, and he had helped her pack and move after

Derek's disappearance. He had suggested she needed a fresh start.

"That weird old radio is being wonky again. Can you take a look at it?"

Corbin smirked, "Sure, thing."

Once inside, the radio was silent. Corbin shrugged, "You're welcome."

She smiled at her own embarrassment.

The only sound was muffled running water.

"There's always something wrong with this old place," she said exasperated. She really missed having Derek around to grease her knobs and tighten her pipes.

Corbin dashed down the hall to the bathroom, only to stop short in the doorway. The sink was overflowing onto the floor with maple-thick, dark blood. Corbin's stomach lurched as he struggled to turn the faucet handles. They remained glued in place. Panic gripped Corbin as he struggled, slipping down the slick, blood-streaked porcelain. He stumbled backward, eyes widening, as he called to Melissa in the other room, "Grab a towel!"

When Melissa appeared in the doorway with a towel in hand, the blood had dried. The empty sink shone glistening white, and the floor was neat and dry.

She caught him staring down at his crimson-stained hands.

"Um... is everything okay?"

Corbin didn't answer. He was agitated, failing to cleanse his hands. Maybe he was tired from helping her move. She'd never seen this side of him.

She needed a moment to breathe; the heaviness in her chest had very little to do with sleep. Losing sleep, replaying once-happy memories, the weight of sorrow pressed against her.

"Let's take a break from unpacking," Melissa sighed as they retired to the living room together. She sat on the couch. He plopped down nearly on top of her.

She hoped for a moment of peace, but knew better than to expect it. Two nights ago, she had a new nightmare. Corbin tore back the floral wallpaper in Melissa's bedroom to reveal oozing scarlet walls. The bedroom furniture had begun to float as she snapped awake to face the same haunted exhaustion she was now desperately trying to escape.

Corbin placed a soothing arm around her. He leaned in close.

They heard a tapping sound. It was a raven trapped inside the glass doors of the fireplace.

"Shoo!" Corbin yelled.

It stared at them with its beady black eyes.

"Deceit! Deceit!" it cawed.

Corbin pushed a small black button, igniting the fireplace with bright yellow and orange flames.

"Stop, Corbin, you'll hurt—"

"Fly out, stupid bird!" he gleefully shouted.

The bird hopped up and flew haphazardly away from the gassy blaze, the ends of its wings sizzling with red embers. With an unsettling flutter, it burst into flames, then vanished into a swirling cloud of black dust.

The faux-mahogany television snapped on.

"—These are their stories. The mysterious cases of 'Unresolved Secrets'!" the host said sternly.

"It's Derek; he's trying to tell me something," Melissa cried, rising from the sofa.

Corbin's eyes widened, his face suddenly gaunt. "Don't be silly."

The flickering glow of the television cast restless shadows

across the wall, twisting Corbin's silhouette into something demonic.

"There must be something wrong with the wiring. I'll figure it out. Go lie down upstairs," he urged, his tone deceptively soft, "you need to rest."

As she hesitated, Corbin's hand shot to the breaker panel, fingers trembling before he yanked the switches down. The house plunged into darkness, the hum of electricity silenced.

"I'm going to the store," he said, grabbing his keys.

Candle in hand, Melissa's feet carried her up the ornate wooden staircase as she heard Corbin's car peel out of the driveway. She found herself in the study, which was filled with the still-packed boxes of her books. On top, she noticed the dog-eared pages of Derek's favorite crime novel, *The Water Cooler Killer*. She flipped it over, reading the blood-red text, summarizing the horror of an office space murder. *A greedy businessman stalks his corporate associates!*

She dropped the book.

Her hand trembled as she parked herself at her desk, grasping her fountain pen. The ink welled up, like the tears behind her eyes. The words *I can't take it anymore*—spilled out onto the fresh, white paper. Her breath trembled in the eerie silence as she scrawled.

She could feel the veil thinning.

An unseen force intervened, preventing her from finishing her dark thought. A phantom hand, maybe death's dark grip, led her away from her desk toward her boudoir.

She froze, a soft whisper hanging in the air, faint but familiar. It was like a breath on the back of her neck, just out of reach. She spun around, her heart racing. Something flickered in the corner of her eye—a shadowy figure in the doorway, watching her. It was a fleeting wisp of smoke that disintegrated in the same shadowy essence as the raven had.

"Derek?" she called out, her voice a hoarse whisper.

Creeeek.

Her stocking-covered feet stepped softly across the hall into the dimly lit bedroom. The air was cool, filled with decades of dust. Her unmade bed lay pressed against the window pane, along with heaps of still-packed boxes.

A plume of black vapor wrapped its arms around her, and a familiar voice filled the air.

"Melissa..." it sighed.

She looked up into the cloud of smoke and saw a man's face staring down at her. It had deep, familiar eyes and a warm, knowing smile.

She stood there bewildered, caught in the warmth of Derek's ghostly embrace. He felt both chilly and comforting, like a brisk February morning. As her mouth hung open in disbelief, his form began to solidify. She shook her head, attempting to erase the vision from her mind like an Etch-A-Sketch.

"Melissa..."

Melissa's heart ached, her eyes welled with tears. Derek reached out a hand, and Melissa felt a comforting chill.

"Honey," Derek urged, his voice desperate. She saw an intensity in his gaze, filled with frustration, pain, and love all tangled up. His expression grew firm, "I need to tell you something..."

Before he could finish, she pressed herself against his cold form like a forgotten fantasy. His eyes frantically searched hers as she cupped his face with her soft hands. Her body ignited with a desire she thought had been lost forever. The cooling comfort of his embrace sent pulsing waves of euphoria through her. His lips tenderly caressed hers.

His kiss was a desperate, raw answer to the hollow ache that had consumed her. His transparent lips rubbed against her warm mouth, a feeling that reminded her of being a little girl, chasing down an ice cream truck, the taste of a frozen popsicle dripping against her eager tongue under the sweltering summer sun.

The fire of her passion swallowed her as she reached for Derek's belt buckle, but her hand couldn't quite grasp it. He lifted her effortlessly by the hips and carried her as he had done across the threshold on their wedding night. But this time, he took her across planes of existence—through time and space, life and death itself—tossing her atop the mattress.

He knelt to the floor at her feet, gathering the waist of her jeans in his hands and pushing it down over her warm thighs in one exhilarating movement. The shock and joy of her pleasure was intensified by the alternating sensation of hot and cold.

Once she was satisfied, he thrust himself upon her, and for the first time in forever, they fell into each other. Their bodies intertwined deeper than they ever had before. His presence moved through her in a way no mortal form could, and her hips quivered with a humming pleasure that revived the deepest parts of her very soul.

As they lay covered in sweat-dripping euphoria, his arms wrapped around her. Then he slowly began covering her face, arms, and neck in frosty kisses. One for every broken part of her, as if to seal in all the healing they had completed.

Then, her mind turned to that fateful night. The moment she lost him...

"I can't bear to lose you again," her eyes pleading for him to stay.

Derek gazed back at her, his heart heavy. "Melissa, I didn't just disappear on you. Something happened to me—" His voice dropped, "I was at the office... I recall a..."

Melissa's breath hitched, a memory flashed. Corbin's desk. "A metal raven paperweight!"

She searched around until she found it and tore open the box labeled *Derek's Office.*

The contents included loose papers, faded receipts, and a leather-bound ledger.

Her eyes scanned the figures. The company wasn't bankrupt; it was thriving, worth millions!

Corbin had warned her that the business was belly-up, that Derek saw the end coming, and likely chose to beat it there. Corbin urged her to sell the maple grove, calling it "dead weight." He even *generously* offered to buy out her inherited share.

She felt a flame of determination ignite inside of her.

She met Derek's eyes, the same eyes she had loved in life and refused to lose in death. "He's not going to get away with this."

The doorknob in the downstairs foyer squeaked.

Melissa descended the steps slowly, carrying the ledger. Corbin met her halfway, his visage lit with quiet rage in the candlelight. "Where did you find that? Give it to me!"

He snatched the document, forcing her back. Her back struck the step. She kicked him in the face. He staggered, bloody-faced, pulling a gun from his belt.

He aimed.

The candle's flame erupted into a pillar of smoke with Derek's smouldering face.

"No! You're dead!" Corbin screamed, eyes wild. He staggered back, falling down the stairs. He crashed into the marble ledge.

Blood oozed out of his lying lips.

"It's over," Melissa whispered to herself.

She felt Derek's cool embrace wrap around her in sweet comfort.

Fio LeFey

Fio LeFey is a paranormal romance author from Salt Lake City. After attending Westminster College, she honed her writing and editing skills as a grant writer in the non-profit world before transitioning to a full-time career as a fiction editor and author. She is a member of the League of Utah Writers' Romance Chapter as well as being the League's Grant Writer. When she's not writing, you can find her at Lovebound Library, Utah's first romance only bookstore. If you are in the mood for something campy and unique, be sure to ask her for a recommendation on your next visit. Follow her on Instagram and TikTok at @cupids.inkwell for updates on her writing, editorial services, and general bookish goodness.

Jasmine Simpson

Jasmine Simpson lived in Nebraska before moving to Utah in 2015. She crafts science fiction, dark fantasy, and speculative short stories, immersing readers in eerie, vivid worlds. Her creativity sparks late at night, guided by moody music, a cup of warm tea, and the moonlight filtering through her window.

Jonathan Reddoch

Jonathan Reddoch is co-owner of Collective Tales Publishing. He is a father, writer, editor, and publisher. He writes sci-fi, fantasy, romance, and especially horror. He's a prolific flash fiction author, but also writes poetry and short stories. He's from southern California, but lives in Salt Lake City. Find him on Instagram @JonathanReddochAuthor or CTPfiction.com

Scarlett Xavier

Scarlett Xavier (she/her) is a steamy romance author bringing the heat one story at a time. Known for her sizzling plots, emotionally charged characters, and happily-ever-afters with bite, Scarlett writes the kind of books you sneak off to read—and never forget. When she's not plotting her next scandalous scene, she's indulging in good coffee, bad reality TV, and dreams that always end in desire. Her upcoming series promises passion, tension, and enough heat to fog up your Kindle.

Stella Taryn

Stella Taryn is a contemporary romance author, avid reader, and former Taco Bell employee of the month. Showcasing her fierce belief in the power of stories to excite, inspire, and challenge, her work features relatable, swoonworthy characters who ultimately find love through deep healing and courageous vulnerability. She lives in southern Utah.

Michaela Rae

Michaela Rae is an emerging author with a rich background in English Literature and Multimedia Design from the University of Utah. She began her storytelling journey by authoring grants and creating marketing materials for the nonprofit sector. Michaela excels at crafting compelling content, a skill she now channels into her speculative fiction, which explores complex themes of power imbalances and overcoming adversity. Residing in a historic bungalow in the heart of Salt Lake City, she also enjoys photography, spending time with her family, and advocating for equity in her community.

Mae Thorn

Mae Thorn writes historical romance, fantasy, and horror. She has published three historical romance books: *Notorious, Dangerous,* and *Rebellious.* Her newest book, *Without Words,* is a historical romance fantasy. Mae holds a Bachelor's degree in English from the University of Utah and a Master's degree in Library and Information Science from San Jose State University. She is the co-president of the League of Utah Writers Romance Chapter, and she lives near Salt Lake City, Utah with her cats; Church, Shadow Moon, and Sabrina, and a puppy, Whiskey.

Sara Fitzgerald

Sara Fitzgerald was named Writer of the Year by The League of Utah Writers in 2006. She is an award-winning author and is multi-published. Sara is an artist who uses splashes of color and magic to create captivating paintings. Her talent has been recognized with the 2023 Connect Winner of the Year award. Her artwork has been displayed for sale at prestigious galleries such as the Urban Arts Gallery in downtown Salt Lake City and the Art Cottage in Gardner Village. Sara lives with her husband and daughter in Salt Lake City. She loves writing, watercolor painting, walking Glitter, her dog, and spending time with her family and loved ones.

Kayla Hansen

Kayla is a Shakespeare fanatic. Give her a quote, she can tell you which play it's from. In her university years, she studied theatre with a focus on directing while harboring a deeper desire to write fiction. Creative writing has followed her through every endeavor, there for her after a long night like a comforting mug of earl grey tea. Working at Disneyland in her early twenties further invigorated her yearning to tell stories of fantastical worlds and magic. Whenever she needed motivation, she remembered meeting Tracy Hickman (writer of Dragonlance) as a young teen and his encouragement to never stop writing. It always led her back to the pages. She is one of the authors of the Pantracia Chronicles, a thirteen-book Romantasy series, and currently lives in Utah with her husband and two fur-babies.

Debra Birdwell Winkler

Debra Birdwell Winkler is a published author who is passionate about sharing her stories. As a former history teacher, Debra weaves historical events into her stories as well as music. She is originally from the South but is now settled in Utah and a member of the League of Utah Writers. Her debut novel, *Cycle of Coincidence*, was released in 2022. Several of her short stories have been published online and in anthologies. She was nominated for the 2022 Best of the Net NonFiction Award and, at the 2024 LUW Quills Conference, she was awarded 3rd place in the League's Annual Creative Writing Romance Short Story Contest. This short story is also published in the September 2024 online magazine, *Ariel Chart International Literary Journal*. Debra is a member of Romance Writers of America and the League of Utah Writers Romance Chapter.

Iris Moonflower

Iris Moonflower is a poet and emerging romantsy writer based in the Salt Lake Valley of Utah. She's dreamed of being a writer since the first grade, when she penned her very first story starring an original character alongside Hook's Rufio. Her writing debut began with a poem published in her high school's literary magazine, and *From Now Until Forever* marks her first official release. A lifelong lover of storytelling, reading, cosplaying, and roleplaying, Iris draws inspiration from the vibrant communities around her. She is currently hard at work on her first full-length fantasy novel, set to release within the next year.

Keyra K. Allred

Keyra K. Allred, native of nowhere, wanderer of Planet Earth, linguaphile, unquenchable reader, photographer, connoisseur of Sapphic ships, both real and strung along for five seasons (looking at you, *Supercorp*), all-consuming lover of all animals, and eater of nachos, seeks to upend erroneous assumptions, bringing the experience of a good love story to heal souls, even if the background includes dragons, ghosts, or corporate evildoers. Three-time "Best of" winner for short story anthologies for the League of Utah Writers Romance Chapter, Keyra plans to do so much more in novel form. Each of the disparate genres calling to them from their laptop documents folder have one very important thing in common: Love. Forever encouraged by their ironically brilliant and bemused husband, Richard, and a Radiant kitten, their plan is to share stories of love, romance, healing, and always, *always*, sarcasm with the world.